VOL. 3, NO. 2   **ISSUE #10**

FEATURES

NEW STORIES

CLASSIC REPRINT

FROM THE CAT'S PERCH

As I write this, the world is slowly recovering from a pandemic that saw many of us staying home—sometimes by choice, sometimes not. Conventions were cancelled or moved online, severely limiting opportunities to gather with other mystery readers, writers, editors, and publishers.

Though I have attended or participated in many formal and informal online events during the past year and a half, Zoom meetings can't replace in-person events. The unplanned hallway conversations, the planned and impromptu meals in the company of other members of our mystery community, rubbing elbows in the bar (even if we don't drink!), and the late-night poker games can't be replicated online.

I attended the 2002 Austin Bouchercon and the 2011 Santa Fe Left Coast Crime, but I did not begin attending mystery conventions on a regular basis until my wife and I attended the New Orleans Bouchercon in 2016. We have attended every Bouchercon since then, and I attended Malice Domestic with Temple in 2018 and alone in 2019. By attending these conventions, I've met many of the editors and publishers with whom I work. I have also met several *Black Cat Mystery Magazine* contributors as well as contributors to the various anthologies I've edited.

Temple and I look forward to the return of in-person events, and have optimistically registered for Malice Domestic and Bouchercon in 2022. If you see us at either of these conventions, or at any other event, please introduce yourself. We'll be glad you did.

—Michael Bracken
Editor, *Black Cat Mystery Magazine*

Staff

PUBLISHER & EXECUTIVE EDITOR
John Gregory Betancourt

EDITOR
Michael Bracken

WILDSIDE PRESS SUBSCRIPTION SERVICES
Karl Würf

PRODUCTION TEAM
Sam Hogan
Karl Würf

THE LAST GASP

H.K. SLADE

Senior Detective Ambrose Broyhill kicked open the door of his unmarked, and the sticky summer heat poured in like swamp water. Instantly, his shirt stuck to his skin, and he felt his eyebrows catch an errant drop of sweat.

"Humph," he grunted as he hefted his great bulk out of the car. The old detective thought, *This is a younger man's game.* And normally it was, but with three gang-related shootings already that morning, the most senior member of the homicide squad was the only investigator free to respond.

Bright yellow crime scene tape sagged under the summer heat. A single patrol officer manned the perimeter, a rookie the same age as Broyhill's grandson. That, even more than Broyhill's personal presence, spoke to just how thinly stretched they were.

A murder scene like this should have a dozen cops, he thought and mopped his forehead with his shirtsleeve. *It's getting scary how few of us are left.*

"Just you?" he asked the young officer. Broyhill nearly had to shout to be heard over the yapping dog in the next-door neighbor's garage. The kid stepped out of his shady spot on the porch and squinted at the glare of the midmorning sun.

"Um, no sir, Detective Broyhill. Officer Hampton is in the house with the body. And the suspect."

Broyhill raised an eyebrow but didn't waste time hassling the kid. *Did his voice actually crack?* Better to just get inside and talk to Friday. Protocol said an officer shouldn't be by herself with a murder suspect, but Officer Friday Hampton grew up under the tutelage of her father, the great Tony Hampton. The young prodigy knew what she was about.

Death had a smell, and after thirty years on the job, Broyhill was a connoisseur. He knew the stink of a victim who had defecated themselves in their last moments of terror, knew how different it was from the putrid stench of a week-old corpse. The tiny house smelled, if not fresh, almost as if nothing were wrong at all. If it hadn't been for the body lying face up in the middle of the room, he'd have bet money his skillset wouldn't be needed.

"What do you got, Friday?" he asked the weary patrol officer standing between the corpse and the handcuffed man slouching on the couch.

"I am glad to see you, Detective," the young woman said. The relief in her voice spilled out like water topping a flooded dam. "I didn't think they were going to be able to send anybody, and I don't know if I'm up to a full murder investigation all on my lonesome."

Broyhill was used to that, used to other people setting their problems on his shoulders. He'd been lucky so far, lucky to hold up under the strain for the better part of three decades. In his secret heart of hearts, though, he longed for the day when he wouldn't have to carry that burden, wouldn't have to be the dead's final hope for justice. *Until the young bucks learned the ropes,* he thought, *I have to stay with it.*

"Don't sell yourself short," he told Friday and put her at ease with a nod.

The detective took notice of the changes in the young woman since the last time he'd seen her. Leaner, wearier, generally more ... seasoned. "The way I hear it, you're a regular crimefighter. Why don't you tell me what you know, and we'll take it from there?"

She pointed to the man sitting on the couch. "This is Sebastian. His English is worse than my Spanish, and I don't speak any Spanish. I wouldn't even know his name except that I found a Honduran ID on him. No wants or warrants. No record at all. The odds of him being a legal immigrant are fifty to one against. He's the only person here besides you, me, and the room-temperature fella on the floor over there."

The man on the couch raised his head at the sound of his name, but nothing in his demeanor nor in his expression indicated he'd understood another word they'd said.

Friday pointed behind Broyhill to the cracked doorframe. "I had to kick the door when I saw the body through the front window. The whole house was locked tight."

"Translator?" Broyhill asked.

Friday shook her head, her tight braid barely moving. "Gomez is tied up at the hospital on that shooting. Rodriguez is at the jail. You see how it is out there."

As if to accentuate her point, her radio blared an emergency tone as the dispatcher announced an armed robbery in progress. Clearly frustrated at not being able to respond, Friday frowned and dialed down the volume to a low murmur.

Broyhill had the man on the couch lean forward so he could look at his hands and asked, "What about that corporal on your squad? What's her name? Sommarriba?"

"She quit two months ago. Couldn't take the nights and weekends anymore. Went to work for a bank."

And the thin blue line grows thinner, Broyhill said to himself, then squashed the thought before it reached his face. *These young officers don't need to see an old man like me wallowing. Already enough despair going around.*

He studied the house. Cheaply built and worn around the edges, but for all that, neat. The couch and the coffee table looked second-hand, the room's single floor lamp one of the cheap Walmart models. Oddly, almost uniquely, the room didn't have a television. In its place hung a framed portrait of the Virgin Mary.

Something yellow/green beneath the couch caught Broyhill's attention. He bent down to retrieve it, a maneuver complicated by both his paunch and his concern that the suspect might try to kick him. Luckily, neither was an issue this time. Broyhill pulled a tennis ball from under the couch, its felt matted and dirty.

He held it up for Sebastian to examine. The man shook his head, either denying ownership of the ball or simply not understanding the situation.

"What brought you here in the first place?" Broyhill asked Friday and tossed the tennis ball to her.

She snatched it out of the air, looked at it, and tossed back. "Nine-one-one hang up. You know, the type that turns out to be nothing a hundred times out of a hundred? I guess it's only ninety-nine times out of a hundred, now."

The man on the couch rocked to one side, presumably to alleviate the discomfort of sitting on the lumpy couch for so long, but his eyes never left his own feet. Broyhill waved the tennis ball at him.

"I suppose there is a good reason Sebastian here isn't in the back seat of your patrol car?"

Friday shrugged, her body armor rising up like a turtle's shell to touch her angular chin. "If I book him, guilty or not, they're going to deport him, and I have this thing about not arresting innocent people. If I can be one-hundred percent honest with you, detective, I just don't think he's our killer."

That caught Broyhill's attention. A gut feeling wasn't proof, but only the most arrogant of detectives ignored a street cop's instincts, especially when she'd been on scene for an hour longer than him.

"Why's that?" he asked as he continued his examination of the crime scene.

"Too calm. I woke him up when I broke down the door, I'd sure of it. He didn't try to run or fight, he just let me cuff him. He didn't seem surprised by the body, though. More sad, if I had to put a name to it."

Broyhill stepped over to the body in question. Hispanic male, mid-twenties, five feet five inches, one hundred thirty pounds. The dead man lay flat on his back on the scratched and dented hardwood floors of the living room, almost as if he'd been laid out for a funeral. A two-inch incision marred the dead center of his bare chest, right on his sternum. His feet, also bare, stretched out across the transition to the kitchen. The toenails were trimmed, but his soles bore the hard callouses of a laborer. The ones on his hands formed a matching set. Other than the obvious wound to his chest, Broyhill couldn't find a single injury. There wasn't even much blood. Barely a trickle.

"No defensive wounds at all," he said aloud.

"I noticed that," Friday agreed, coming to stand beside him. "The murder weapon is that giant-horking-knife on the kitchen floor. I can't imagine someone sticking him like that without him wanting to do something about it. It's almost like the murderer found him sleeping. Even then, you'd think he'd jolt awake, right? It's a head scratcher."

Broyhill wandered into the kitchen. Most of the cabinets had doors, but not all. The counters practically sagged under the weight of rice, two-liter sodas, and prepackaged meals bought in bulk from the shopping club down the street. The appliances looked older than the officer outside, the dents and dings touched up with housepaint wherever the white enamel had cracked. The refrigerator, sitting just inside the kitchen, had a coin-sized dent that was too new to have received the paint treatment but hadn't yet rusted. The old

Frigidaire hummed and clanked as the compressor fan glanced off something internally.

The knife in question lay on the warped vinyl flooring, a non-serrated, full-tang carving knife. Two sets of nuts and bolts held its aftermarket wooden handle together, still-wet blood covering the final four-inches of its ten-inch blade. Broyhill looked back at the seemingly fatal wound on the decedent.

"Right?" Friday said, reading his thoughts. "The amount of force it would take to drive Frankenstein's meat cleaver though this guy's chest plate like that … somebody was motivated. Or had a running start."

Broyhill had his suspicions. The facts were already beginning to coalesce into a blurry picture, but he knew better than to let his suspicions steer the investigation. That's what facts were for. So many young investigators confused the two.

"Your old man enjoying retirement?" he asked Friday. "Is his knee still bothering him?"

His old friend's daughter stood silhouetted in the dusty sunlight streaming through the plastic blinds, her hands hooked into the neck of her vest to let some of the heat out. "No, the knee doesn't bother him at all anymore," she said. "He passed away back in January."

Broyhill stopped in tracks, and some of his strength drained away. "I just saw him at Christmas. He only retired a year ago. What happened?"

"Heart attack. It's been tough, but I can't say it was a total surprise. No exercise, bad food, smoked for half his life … and you know how much he lived this job. I think when he stopped being a cop, he lost his purpose for getting up every day."

That hit home. Broyhill wanted to say something, to tell her how much he thought of her old man. Before he could get the words out, Friday's radio crackled to life, stealing the moment. A multiple vehicle crash on the far side of town and no one to answer.

Broyhill cleared his throat. Words weren't going to do a damn thing. The best he could do was help Tony's daughter wrap up this mess and maybe teach her a thing or two.

"I guess we better see if we can figure this out so you can get back in the fight," he said. "Step into the bedrooms and tell me what you notice. I'll keep an eye on our friend Sebastian here."

Friday squinted at him suspiciously. "Anything in particular you want me to look for?"

It was such a patrol officer way of thinking. *Tell me what to do and how to do it.* They needed a process to follow. A good investigator, however, looked at the world differently. "The opposite," he told her. "Forget about whatever you think happened here and just see what catches your eye."

Friday shrugged and set off on her task. Broyhill stood in the middle of the living room and let his mind wander back to his younger days. He should have been focused on the task at hand, but more and more he found that he didn't have as much of a say in where his mind went as he did when he was young and full of piss and vinegar.

This house was just down the road from the Sunny Acres Trailer Park where, twenty-five years ago, the South Side Rolling Twenties had spent half a year terrorizing the residents. He and Tony Hampton had rolled hard and heavy trying to catch the punks before someone got hurt. It hadn't been enough. After the old man turned up in the park beaten half to death, the two young cops had spent a cold, miserable night standing in the rain, wrapped in their black rubber slickers and the type of inky darkness only found in truly poor neighborhoods.

After a few hours of shivering in the dark with nothing to show for it, Tony had gone off to take a leak and left Broyhill leaning in the dubious shelter of a rusted trailer. Rain ran down the neck of his slicker and trickled behind his vest. He closed his eyes just for a moment and blew into his hands to warm them. When he opened his eyes again, he was staring down the barrel of a Saturday night special, on the other end of which was a young Southsider eager to wear the mantle of a cop killer. Broyhill couldn't move, couldn't even breathe. The world went quiet except for the sound of the snap breaking on a departmentally issued holster and Tony's slow, southern drawl from somewhere in the darkness: "Either that gun goes in the dirt or you do. Make a decision, Hoss."

Now Tony was dead, his watch ended, and Broyhill wasn't that far behind. He held no illusions how long he'd make it as a retiree. The sun was setting on their day. *Who'll remember us and all our adventures when I'm gone?* he thought. *Little Friday? Sebastian here?*

The handcuffed man looked up at him, his thick, black eyebrows arched in an unspoken plea. Broyhill looked him directly in the eyes, trying to decide if he was looking at a murderer or an innocent man.

Friday emerged from the back hallway, notepad in hand, interrupting the detective's ruminations.

"How many bedrooms?" Broyhill asked, trying to shake off his melancholy.

"Two," Friday said, all business. "One with the bed made, the other just a mattress and a bundle of sheets."

"What's that tell you?"

"The mattress probably belongs to Sebastian. Like I said, I woke him up. That means the other probably belongs to our victim. Unless he's Sebastian's overnight guest, which is unlikely given that there's a cellphone, wallet, and pair of work boots in the other room that look to be a good fit for our Juan Doe."

"Money?" Broyhill asked. *Always an important point to clear up.*

"Someone cleaned out the wallet. Thoroughly. The leather was still stretched out from holding cards and cash." Friday slapped her open palm with her notepad. "If it was a robbery, though, I don't get the made bed. Or why they left the gold necklace I found hanging on a hook by the door."

Broyhill nodded his approval of the young officer's observation. *Interesting, but not unexpected,* he thought. "Was there a cross on the necklace?"

"Of course. And a rosary."

"Anything else?"

She shrugged. "I didn't want to try the passcode on the phone and jack things up. There was a Western Union Money Transfer folded up all nice and crisp in a dogeared Spanish Bible on the nightstand, though." Friday flipped a page back in her notebook. "Going to one Vanessa Perez in Antigua Guatemala, Guatemala. Just a skosh under a grand, dated this morning from the Stop and Rob on the corner."

"Anything in the hallway?"

Instead of just answering, Friday looked back over her shoulder to see if Broyhill could have seen down the hall from where he was standing. "Funny that you ask," she said slowly. "There's a leather tool belt. Nice one. Seen a lot of use, but it's quality and in good shape."

"And the tools? Wrenches and screwdrivers or a hammer and tape measure?" He knew the answer, but he was trying to walk the young officer down the path.

She didn't look or check her notepad, but recited from memory. "Hammer. Tape measure. Speed square. That sort of thing."

Broyhill used the drier of his two sleeves to dab the sweat from his forehead. He had enough now. *But did Friday?* Next time, he might not be there, and then who would speak for the dead? *The kid outside who probably didn't need to shave before going on duty this morning?*

Sighing, Broyhill asked, "Have you figured it out yet, Officer Hampton?"

"Figured what out?" she snapped, clearly impatient with Broyhill's method of teaching. "The murder? With all due respect detective, are you insane? We need the crime scene techs. Fingerprints, DNA, the medical examiner's people. This isn't some locked room mystery you can solve by just looking at things like Sherlock Holmes."

"Hmm," Broyhill hummed. "Isn't it?"

Her attitude was typical of anyone who grew up watching shows like *CSI* and *Bones*; they expected all the breaks to come from some man in a lab coat or a woman permanently installed behind a set of flatscreen monitors. Technology had robbed a generation of cops of their ability to piece together their own observations.

"Tell your partner to head next door and start a canvass," Broyhill told her. "Ask them when the last time they saw Mr. Perez was. And see if anyone speaks Spanish. We'll need to get Sebastian here to corroborate a few things before we can let him go."

Friday set her arms on her hips and narrowed her eyes. "Let him go?"

The big detective met her level gaze. She had a hard stare, just like her old man, but not as good as Broyhill's. His had the weight of experience behind it.

Friday took a deep breath, and Broyhill saw the gears turning in her head. She was frustrated by the heat and the workload and the calls for help that she couldn't answer, but she recognized that the old detective didn't get to where he was by being stupid. Tony's daughter was a good cop, and that meant she wanted to be a better one.

"OK, you lost me," she finally admitted. "What am I missing?"

Loosening his already loose tie, Broyhill rewarded her with a smile that stretched out his bushy mustache. "It's all in the hands, Friday. Have your partner get started, then take a look at Sebastian's paws and tell me what you see."

She did. Sebastian said something meek in Spanish which Broyhill took to be an offer to let them look at his hands all they wanted if they would take the cuffs off. Friday just had him lean forward.

"No scratches," she confirmed. "There's a cut on his left palm, but it's old. Nothing under the fingernails but dirt."

"What kind of dirt?"

She thought about it, then looked again. "Grease, maybe? There's more grease stains in the creases of his knuckles."

"Correct. What does that tell you?"

"I don't know." She let Sebastian lean back and stood up straight. "Could be anything."

"Not just anything," Broyhill corrected her. "What if I bet you a ten-dollar bill that when you look in his closet, you'll find a mechanic's shirt? Probably gray or blue with his name embroidered on a little oval patch on the chest."

"I wouldn't bet against you, detective, but I don't know what that has to do with anything."

Broyhill tapped the side of his head. "What's an auto mechanic doing with a nice set of carpenter's tools? And why would they be outside his door? And if it was a side hustle for Sebastian, wouldn't he be out working on a day like today? No, the only carpenter in this house is the dead one over here. Mr. Perez."

"Are you sure?"

"Look at the hands. You tell me."

Friday crossed the room and knelt down to study the dead man's hands. "Nothing under the nails. One of them has a blood blister. Probably smacked it pretty good a month or so ago."

"Occupational hazard for a carpenter. You notice anything else?"

"He's married. Or used to be. No ring, but that dent on his left ring finger says there was. The hands are clean. Scrubbed, even. There is something, though, right on the back. Like someone drew a little picture in green Sharpie."

The arm of the couch creaked precariously as the detective took a seat on it. He nodded to Friday. "It's an ink stamp. A butterfly. It means Mr. Perez went to Xenon last night."

Friday's eyebrows knitted together. "Xenon? The gay bar downtown? Are you thinking the killer followed him home? Maybe a jealous boyfriend?"

If only it were that easy, he thought. He only knew the stamp because he'd worked cases involving Xenon before. The bar had an excellent camera system and the owners were always happy to help the police protect their customers. "No. Someone came home with him last night, but that man's long gone. The killer is still in the house."

The young officer bristled. "I searched the house before you got here, detective. I'll stake my reputation that this place is clear."

A lopsided grin lifted one edge of Broyhill's mustache. "No need to get your hackles up, Friday. I wasn't questioning your ability. The opposite, really. You've got all four corners of this puzzle pieced together and most of the edges. You're doing better than half the detectives in the division these days."

She relaxed into the patrolman's stance: thumbs hooked behind her belt buckle, feet shoulder-width apart, elbows resting on her gun and radio, respectively. "Care to help me fill in the middle?" she asked.

Broyhill laid it out. "Mr. Perez here isn't going to come back as a citizen of these United States. Most likely, he's only been in the country for a couple months to judge by his shopping habits. He bought in bulk, see? Where he grew up, you only went into town once a month or so. He was raised a good Catholic boy. Left his family behind to come to America and make some money. We'll probably find he works with a family member, an uncle or a cousin, someone who cares enough about him to hand him down that toolbelt."

Friday nodded. "Makes sense. I'm tracking so far."

"Yesterday was payday. Mr. Perez ... was probably very lonely. He went downtown to seek some comfort there, as the song goes. He met someone, some-one who wasn't his wife. Someone, crucially, who wasn't a woman. They came home together. Spent the night together. And then his new companion left Mr. Perez alone. Alone with his Bible and his wedding ring and the crushing guilt of having not only broken his holy vow, but having sinned against God. At least according to his beliefs." Broyhill bit his lip and pointed up at the portrait of the Virgin Mother. If he was right, it was the last face in this world the decedent had seen.

Friday stood up from where she had been kneeling and followed the detec-tive's gesture. "You think he killed himself?" she asked. "Isn't that a sin, too?"

Broyhill couldn't take the heat anymore. He unbuttoned his sleeves and began rolling the cuffs up. "You've been around the block a few times by now," he said. "Haven't you ever seen someone so deep in a hole they think their only way out is by digging?"

She crossed her arms and shook her head. "There's no way he pushed that knife through his chest like that."

"Take a look at the dent on the fridge. The fresh one."

Friday looked. "What about it?"

"See the height? That match up with anything else you recognize?"

Looking down at the corpse, Friday Hampton did the math. The dent matched up almost perfectly with the chest wound. "No...." she said, not want-ing to believe what the evidence was telling her.

"Yes," Broyhill assured her. "Like you said, the killer was highly motivated. Mr. Perez held the knife to his chest and ran at the sturdiest thing he could find. We'll have to wait for the medical examiner's report, but my surmise is that he nicked a ventricle, took a step back, pulled the knife out, then laid down on the floor to die. When we roll him over, we're going to find massive evidence of livor mortis. He bled to death internally. Sebastian here didn't murder anybody. Neither did our victim's new lover. Guilt did it for Mr. Perez. Guilt and despair."

Friday looked at Broyhill as if he had just relayed a message from a ghost. "There's no way, *no way* you could know all that."

"It's right here in front of us. The check to his wife? That was his entire savings. He knew he wasn't going to have any use for it anymore. Same thing with his tools. Made his bed and folded his clothes so someone else could use them."

"I didn't say he folded his clothes." It came out like an accusation.

"Were they folded?" Broyhill asked, and didn't bother to hide the slight reproach in his tone.

"Yes," she grudgingly admitted. "In neat stacks on the floor. But that can't be it. There are lots of possible explanations for all that. You can't be so certain."

He tossed the tennis ball to her. "What do you smell?"

"Nothing." She sniffed. "Nothing unusual."

She probably thinks I'm talking about weed, Broyhill figured. *Patrol officer thinking*.

"That musty smell, right at the edge of your nose? That's the smell of a dog. Mr. Perez's dog. The one in the garage next door. And that's his slobber all over that ball. The dog's, not Mr. Perez's. Though if it is his, this case is going to get a lot more interesting."

At that moment, the young officer returned from his canvass. Sweat rings outlining the armpits of his still perfectly tailored uniform. He knocked on the open door like he'd been called to the principal's office.

"What did they say?" Friday asked him.

"The lady next door said the dog belongs to the guy who lives here, Dante Perez. He came by around eight this morning and gave her the dog and food and a bunch of toys. She said he looked weird. She was worried but didn't know who to call."

Detective Broyhill nodded. "A man like the late Mr. Perez doesn't get rid of his dog lightly," he explained to Friday. "Everything about him says he'd want the pup taken care of, though. Is the puzzle coming together for you now?"

She tossed the ball back to Broyhill. "Damn sad."

"That it is. But at least we can do one good thing, now. Why don't you uncuff our friend Sebastian? I'll wait with him for the medical examiner so you kids can get back to saving the world."

"Are you sure?" Friday asked, though she already had her cuff key in her hand.

"I'm sure," he told her. There wasn't anything more here for him to teach the young officer. This wouldn't be his first time waiting with a dead body, or even his hundredth. Maybe it would be his last, though. He waved for Friday to get going. "The city needs you a lot more than it needs a fat old cop like me."

"I wouldn't say that, detective. I wouldn't say that at all."

✗

H.K. Slade is a writer specializing in police procedurals set in eastern North Carolina. You can find his previously published works in *Mystery Weekly, Everyday Fiction, Allegory Magazine,* and *Alien Skin,* as well as on his own website: hkslade.com.

SPOOK

EMILIO DEGRAZIA

Everything was mute and calm; everything gray.... Shadows present,
foreshadowing deeper shadows to come.

—Herman Melville, *Benito Cereno*

Monday morning talk left me troubled and confused. They say Rondel Collins, the black nineteen-year-old we think of as the one who killed Ginny Gunderson right here in Chisolm on Saturday night, was cornered in a barn way down in Alabama. We didn't know his name until Ginny hit the news. The latest word is that Collins holed himself up in one of the barn's stalls. The police shot in self-defense because they didn't know what he'd do when he didn't come out with his hands in the air. They said they had no way of knowing who he was or where he was from, and they said they couldn't be sure he didn't have a gun or a knife when they went in after him. Here I am, in a small Minnesota Iron Range town more than a thousand miles away, wondering if it was somebody else who died in that Alabama barn. What I wonder is how he had it in him to get from Chisolm on Saturday to Alabama in time to get shot. There are too many miles and not enough hours for somebody named Rondel Collins to get himself killed on a Sunday that far away.

I don't think the fastest car on the planet would have gotten him to that barn in time. Ginny Gunderson's old boyfriend Jason had a car, the old clunker Ford I saw in back of Bert's video store. But I never saw Collins in a car. I don't know of any train he could hop to get himself that far away that fast, and Collins was big enough I can't see him flying there on his own. I figure he's on his way back to hide out in some big city like Detroit, where he told Ginny he's from. For sure now we'll never see him alive or dead again, except maybe when we're looking at some new black stranger who shows up on a Chisolm street.

I think there's been a terrible mistake because I think I saw Collins just outside of Chisholm on Sunday night.

People don't get stabbed to death in Chisholm every day, not even once a year. So people in towns like ours get heated up when something terrible like this happens, even in winter when they turn their backs to each other to fish in frozen lakes. There the fishing shacks get a slick on their floors from the silences breathed out by townies every hour they spend humped over holes thinking while they're waiting for a fish to show enough nose to break the ice. A lot of good folk in these parts like the peace and quiet of their cabins and fishing holes, being left alone just to mind their own business there.

When something terrible like a murder happens and we see the name of our town in somebody else's news, we get excited for a week or two because it puts us on somebody's map. Here we have a black outsider from Detroit doing a horrible thing to one of our own pretty girls. For once it means we're suddenly big enough for something like that happening every day in a big city like Detroit. But we also want everybody to know we're not Detroit. We want Detroit's troubles to steer clear of us, go away someplace else. If a drifter from Detroit stabs his girlfriend in the chest, he stabs every one of us.

Detroit wasn't on my mind when I drove out to Julian's old farm. Julian takes a couple weeks off in January to sell his paintings in New Mexico, and that's where I come in on Sunday nights. His water pipes like to freeze up when he's gone south. It's my job to keep the water moving in those pipes and the furnace running so Julian's farmhouse is still alive when he gets home from New Mexico.

So on Sunday night I put my book down, say goodnight to my wife Judy as she trundles up to bed, and I head out into the dark and cold. Saturday brought us the murder and then five inches of snow, one of those pure white blankets that gets a hard crust when the sub-zeros blow over it. What I see is all that snow and ice, but what I'm thinking about is the thing that happened on Saturday night we don't know how to think about, with most of us clammed up like the cold outside, not knowing what to say or not saying what we think we believe. The windshield is white with those designs that get frozen stiff when I breathe out, and I'm seeing Ginny Gunderson in her bed in those white designs, the bloody mess made of her there, with the black man who's been hanging out with her gone after she's found dead in that bed, with him just disappeared somewhere out there in the dark.

I'm lucky the car starts and the roads are cold enough for the tires to stick to them. My drive to Julian's farm is fine until a wheel slips into the rut on the driveway leading to his house. Luckily I back out of the rut, but that's as far as I get with the car. I have to walk the last fifty yards to Julian's front door.

It's a clear night, the air sharp on my face. Even with a full moon rising above the trees, the sky is blazing with so many stars it makes you shudder to think about how deep the mysteries way out there get. The night is quiet and still except for the racket I make as I trudge toward the house, cracking my way through the crust and sinking in about a half-foot with each step. In the moonlight I see a wide field of white surrounding the house, no sidewalk or path, no footprints to walk in to keep myself from stepping in some hole with a quicksand so white there's maybe no bottom to it.

I can't say I really notice somebody's car half-buried in snow next to the chicken coop, because the fence posts, looking like a row of creepy white-hooded monks walking off toward the woods make me wonder if I'm seeing ghosts. That car's somebody's old clunker, out of sight the way any useless thing seems gone. I just want to do my little job: Get in, check the faucets, furnace and pipes, and go home to Judy and my own warm bed. I run the chores through my mind: Turn the kitchen faucet on, then check the faucets upstairs, remember to leave the bathtub spigot open just a hair to let a trickle of water out. Then the part I don't like: Open the trapdoor under the kitchen rug, haul myself down the stepladder to the basement, and check the furnace. The pilot light. That's the last thing Julian says before he leaves. Be sure to check the pilot light. He's been having trouble with it. I hate the basement cold and its moldy smell, but I have to go down there to check the pilot light he never bothers to fix.

Only when you get close enough to somebody's house do you find it hard not to look in. From a distance a farmhouse is a lonely thing, easy enough to drive past because nobody ever seems home, and plain enough to make you believe food really comes from the stores. It's only when you're up close that an old farmhouse shows you what's on its mind, and more often than not that mind is tired and falling asleep from hard work. It's not just the kitchen floor sagging under the weight of the wives who spend years lumbering back and forth from sink to stove, or the layers of paint peeling from weather-beaten boards. You see things that never got fixed because nobody had time for them—the roof gutter hanging on by a nail, the shutters all askew, the windows painted shut—and you have half a mind to call the ghosts of farmers back from their graves to set things right. I'm used to the clutter inside Julian's house—the raggy rug and heap of old shoes by the door, the piles of books on the floor, the jackets and pants thrown over the backs of chairs. But some things go so deep you can't just wipe them out, the tobacco stink, for example, that not even winter winds blasting through open windows whitewash away. Farmers smoked in their houses before the roofs went up, and the rooms they lived in got smeared with smoke stains for the next hundred years. Here they all were, those several generations of farm folk who ate, slept, worked, smoked cigarettes, died, and left the ghosts of their odors here.

Before I feel for the key in its usual place under the rubber mat, I put my nose to the window to look in. It's hard to see much of anything except the dirty curtains hanging down, not even the big mirror facing the door, and it only takes a few seconds for my breath to freeze thick enough on the window for the curtains on the other side to disappear. As I'm trying to see through the window I have a crazy thought: What was it like for Ginny Gunderson when she lay there watching herself bleed?

I hold my breath as I bend down to feel for the key. I'm relieved to find it where it belongs, and it slips in easily enough. But my old battle with the door is brand new all over again. I pull the handle in, then out, then lift with half my might, then try again to twist and turn the key in the lock. They're so set in their ways there's no method to the madness of old doors. I step away, blow breath on my freezing hands, then yank again. Nothing. I try lifting the door, and when it won't budge I stare it down then curse the thing and tell the key to snap in the lock and go to hell. Finally I throw my shoulder at the door and step back as the noise I'm making barges into the farmyard and goes nowhere away.

"Damn you!" I scream at the door.

And the door, as if moved by my blast of hot air, opens just enough to let me in.

I close it quietly and stand there in the dark trying to see into the living room. Julian's favorite chair is to my right, the fat sofa is across from it, and the ticking of the old mantel clock seems to get louder as I listen hard. I grope along the wall for the light switch, nervous I'll trip on Julian's clutter. When I flip the switch I find myself next to a rocking chair, with an open book on the seat and Julian's slippers in the middle of the floor. The dining room table is cluttered with dishes and mail, and an old woolen coat is draped over a chair. A broom leans against the wall next to the oak buffet. And across from the mirror on the far dining room wall is the antique portrait he picked up at a farm auction. It's a large dark-framed thing picturing a sour-face from early settlement days, one of those hard-working bearded saints who fathered a dozen children and never wept at the funerals of the half-dozen who got their revenge on their old man by dying of some frontier fever before finishing their chores. Two of him watch me from opposite sides, the one to my right in the dark frame, the other across from him in the mirror.

"Good evening, Moses," I say out loud. I walk past his two-faced self to check out Julian's bedroom. The two versions of Moses follow me as I walk to the bedroom door.

I flick on the light. The bed is unmade, a newspaper off to one side, the wardrobe door open, a few shirts and pants hanging inside. There's a long crack in the wallpaper behind the bed. As I run my eyes along the edge of the crack I see this is not some illness the house suffers because of years of sub-zero temperatures. The crack is as antique as the wallpaper, maybe one of the ways old houses have of reminding us nothing's square enough to stand straight on an earth still round. There's something crazy about the way the crack arches over Julian's bed like a lightning streak, then inches its zigzag way down to a heap of dirty underwear coolly stewing in the far corner of the room. Julian the artist is a slob, and I feel perverse and privileged to have access to his privacy. We two are maybe too much alike, not always what we seem, except he always laughs at his own jokes. I often wonder about his laugh, what sadness is in its noise, and how the disorder of his household works its way into the complex patterns he achieves on the paintings the New Mexico tourists pay good money for. There's too much Julian for me to ever know. I know only that I love his pictures too and like him enough to keep the blood running through his house's veins.

I'd been in the kitchen before so I know I have to prepare myself. The house is cold enough for me to see my breath and keep the stink in the kitchen sink from gagging me. There's a stack of dishes he left to soak for the winter months. Do I do his dishes too? I summon the courage to plunge in with one hand to find the drain. A shiver grabs my spine as the water slowly seeps away, its final gasp a small gurgle in the black hole of the pipe. I turn the faucet on full, and give the sink a general rinse. The dishes will have to compost in the cold until Julian's return.

No frozen water pipes. Next comes the ugly part—the furnace pilot light. I'll just get it over with and then reward myself by visiting the bathroom upstairs.

I don't think much of it—the way the trapdoor rug is heaped to one side of the kitchen floor. There's no hiding the trapdoor under this rug. As I grab the iron ring to lift the door a chunk of ice from the roof comes crashing down on the back porch steps. For a moment I think someone has pounded on the door with a fist, but the darkness inside the trapdoor pit draws me back to the reality of having to descend the precarious ladder on slippery boots. The only basement light, a bare bulb, is to the left of the ladder, its pull chain an old leather shoelace. I'll feel better once I get that piece of leather in my hand.

I descend the steps carefully, relieved to achieve solid dirt under my feet. The dank odor makes itself known, an underground smell of stones that have never seen the sun. A dungeon, filthy and cold. Good wine would rot down here. I find the old leather shoelace and give it a yank.

Nothing happens. Except for the dim shaft of light falling on the ladder from above, I am in the dark. Then the trap door slams shut of its own free will, leaving me there in pitch black.

My good sense tells me to hightail it up the ladder, get the flashlight from my car, and get on with the furnace work. But a chill drifts past my face. Ahead of me in the dark, to the left of the spot where the old furnace squats, I hear a muffled sound of what seems the shuffling of feet, and then the latch of a closing door.

My legs go numb as my heart leaps to attention, its beatings like footsteps running away. I stand still as a stone. There's nowhere to run.

Who is it down here? I tell myself not to be stupid—don't make a move.

I've never seen a ghost or had any good reason to believe in them. The world is strange, wonderful and terrible enough without vague vapors to complicate my nights or the simple tasks Julian asked me to perform. But there's something about standing alone in the dark that erases the line between day and night, here and there, you and me, right and wrong. In the dark all things are equal, and possible, and in that dark I hear feet and a closing door.

"Hello," I say quietly, "are we alone down here?"

I hold my breath to be sure of what I hear next—another movement behind the door, like a person's body slouching down, settling in low behind a wall. This is no cat or raccoon. I stand as still as I can, straining to hear something clearer and more specific, and in the silence I hear my own dark thoughts making no sense to me. Here I am in the dark. There are presences nobody can see, few of them with faces resembling our own. Our senses may fool us, but they prefer not to lie about dangers scheming to do us harm. So why would my senses make a fool of me? They're warning me: Somebody is hiding from you, and the danger is real enough to make you want to hide or run.

I hear my own words: "I'm here for a furnace check."

I hear another muffled movement a few feet from me.

I try seeing it, the door. He's in the coal bin, the little room no longer in use after Julian jerry-rigged the gas burner to the furnace. I had looked inside the coal bin once before, had seen the walls made of rough-cut boards and the pile of leftover coal, with the shovel leaning against the blackened back wall.

He, whoever he was, was in the coal bin, crouching next to the wall, maybe watching me through a small space between the boards. If there were a wisp of light I'd see the whites of his eyes.

Again I try to think: Why is he here, and why now? I had taken enough time to get in the house, had announced my presence in my struggle with the door. He could have greeted me, ushered me in, explained his presence away. Or he could have done the more convenient thing: Slipped out the back door without me knowing it.

I imagine his face blackened by coal dust in the bin. Collins doesn't own a car. He shows his face in town, spends three months coming and going from her place, and he disappears right after she's found dead. The police consider Collins dangerous. He probably has a gun.

Was it really the latch of the coal bin door I heard? Or is he waiting there with his gun?

Looking back now I see that there are a few moments in life, and only a few, when we realize how unexceptional we are. All ambition drains from us then, and fear turns into resignation void of any sense of defeat, even as a certain lightness rises in us, lifting us above ourselves.

But standing there in Julian's basement I don't think about what's obvious: Collins and I are both unexceptional. If I'm trapped down here, so is he, and that makes both of us more dangerous.

Nothing is clear as I stand in the dark, more alert than I ever have been before, more *alive*. The presence behind the coal bin door is leaning against a wall made of old boards, and that wall is just a few inches away, close enough for me to touch with my hand. Above me the trap door opening to the kitchen floor seems like a heavy iron sewer grate I can't find in a black sky, with my legs suddenly so numb under me I can't dream of making a mad dash for the rickety steps.

I remember walking in the woods some months ago—alone there, with no gun, no desire to hunt—when I happened on a doe and her fawn feeding behind a bush, the mother, startled by my presence, standing perfectly still in big-eyed silence, ears on alert as her fawn nibbled at the grass.

Rondel Collins, why wouldn't he have a gun? One day he just happens to show up in our town. The next thing we know he's walking down the street with Jason's girl, Ginny Gunderson. What did she see in him?

I try seeing him, his hand on the door latch, waiting for me to make a move. I remember him in the grocery store, lagging a step behind Ginny as she pushes a cart down the aisle. He's in a hooded sweatshirt, dark green, with white lettering. Just then a little boy pulls away from his mom's hand and stops in the middle of the aisle to stare at him. Collins, a sweatband pulled low over his brow, smirks as he glances down at the boy, as if to say, What are you smiling at with your little blond face? You think I'm a— Then his smirk turns into a wide smile full of white teeth.

Ginny smiles at the boy.

"What's your name?" the boy says just as his mother catches up with him and pulls him away from them.

If he opens the bin door and shows himself, then I would explain I am almost done with the faucets upstairs, that the pilot light would take but a minute or two, and that Judy, my wife, is waiting for me at home. That I want to be with her, not here, with my arms and legs wrapped around her. That between lovers things sometimes go wrong, terribly wrong.

I hear another movement inside the bin. He's near the door, almost on the other side of me, trying to read my mind. He can't decide, wants to know what I'm thinking of doing next.

I put my hand on the coal bin wall. Rough lumber, birch or pine, with prickly grain. I run my hand over the board, seeing him again, the green sweatshirt, a gold ring on his left ear, torn jeans, frayed sneakers, a silver chain around his neck. Is he sweating down here, with the basement stones so cold?

He's no fool. He knows I could play hardball with him, give my argument a final twist: If I'm not home with my wife in the next hour or so, she'll call the police and the first place they'll come looking is here.

I'm also the fool. He could do me in and be gone before anyone finds me here.

I don't come out with the obvious: He can do what he wants to me, but he has no real hope. Where will he go? Where will he hide? Everybody knows what he looks like, and everybody is looking for him.

He stirs uneasily on his side of the wall, and I hear him breathing, slow and deep like a man resigning himself.

I see the hopelessness in that breath: If I turn around and find the steps leading me to the trap door, and if I just leave the house, just go away—where will he go after I'm gone? His footprints in the snow will follow him.

I see footprints leading away, perhaps to somebody's car, a bus or train, and I see his dark form shrinking as it distances itself from the house, a black man disappearing into a night whitened by a thick sheet of snow with nothing on it but prints pointing to some cave, or an empty stall in somebody's barn.

I have some matches in my coat pocket. I just need one to get the pilot light going. I'm afraid to rummage for them. He'll think I'm making a move.

I begin wondering if I'm wrong. Do I have the wrong man in there? When he first appeared in town I started asking around. Anybody know who he is, what he's doing here? "Some black dude from Detroit passing through," is what Cal Smithson said at the Cenex station. So I nod and say yes to myself. He's a black dude from Detroit passing through, somebody with no name.

I hear him shift his weight from one foot to the next, and listen hard for him to make the slightest move toward the door. He clears his throat. The basement air is cold, and it feels heavy, stained by the odor of a man's pants and shirt. I take two steps to my left and as I reach for it the wall gives way like a door opening, dissolves into the darkness we find ourselves in.

He seems just to the left of me now. I search for a face, his eyes.

"Who are you?"

My words hang in the air. I hear him fall back away from me into the corner of the bin where I saw the shovel leaning against the wall. I see him as a lump on the floor, cowering. He's so close I could kick him, but I don't dare let him know my mind: You used the knife on her. You couldn't get her to stay with you or go away with you. You don't belong here and couldn't let go of her. You couldn't just go away, and you'll never be white enough for her. That's what we thought when we just walked past each other and looked at the sidewalk. So she told you to go, just go away, leave her alone. And her old boyfriend Jason was still in town. And you said no, if you couldn't have her, nobody would.

I turn my back on him and feel my way along the coal bin wall and then the furnace finds my hands. It's an old round thing, the ductwork rising out of it like the coils of dragons with their heads buried in the basement joists. I lift the latch of the furnace's iron mask. Dead. Nothing inside but the stench of old ashes and bad basement air.

A black dude from Detroit. That's what he was to me. Nothing but trouble. Somebody with no name, no face. A nobody in the dark.

I grope for the reset button on the gas burner, find the button but can't see the small pilot light. I fumble for the matches in my pocket, look at the wall of the bin to be sure he's not making a move. I strike a match.

As the light flares I hear him behind the door. He stumbles as he tries to stand, then falls back down in the corner where I saw the shovel leaning against the wall.

"I'm going to get this furnace going, so we can have some heat in this house. Then I'm going to make you a deal."

I strike another match, comforted by the sulfurous smell it gives off. I find the reset button with my thumb, set the match to the pilot light. It flares, then gives me a red-blue jet of flame. The furnace switch is on the basement beam to my left. I hit the "On" button.

The house shudders as the furnace kicks in, and the flames inside the furnace's iron grate make it look like an eerie brain on fire.

I go down on one knee just outside the small opening in the coal bin door. If the opening were wider I'd see our heads shadowed on the back wall. He's just inside the door, also crouched low, glaring up at me. I whisper my words through the furnace noise.

So here's the deal: Get the hell out of here. Go someplace else. I walk out of here and go home to my wife. I don't say one word about you. You don't say one word about me. It's after midnight now. I give you twenty-four hours to get the hell out of here, make a dash for it, go away, just go away. I don't say a word.

I don't say what I believe. That he never wanted her dead, that the rage he felt when he picked up the knife drained from him when he saw her suddenly stilled, the rage gone even as he stood looking down at her, her face a stranger's as he gathers his things and walks out the door wondering what next, where do I go, where do I hide, nothing matters any more except the new slow burn twisting itself like the knife into the heart, with the mind whispering, insisting, I didn't do it, I don't know who she is, I didn't do it, no not me. She's somebody else and I'm somebody else. Somebody else killed her. Not me.

I give my argument its final twist: My wife will call the police and they'll come here looking for me. My car's out there, and my footprints lead straight to this house.

Where will you run? Where will you go where nobody will know who you are?

I let my thoughts hang there as I turn my back and take hold of the ladder. I climb up slowly, deliberately, letting him know I'm in control. And when I pull myself up into the kitchen I leave the trapdoor open for him. I still have things to do. I check the faucet in the sink again to make certain that the thin trickle is holding steady. On my way out I poke my head into the bedroom, then switch off the light in the living room. On a table is one of Julian's pieces of art, a pen and ink sketch of a face in black and white.

The door locks when I pull it shut. I let out a deep breath as I stand on the porch looking at the snow stretched smooth all the way to the distant trees. The moon is high overhead, small and bright in the sky, its light spreading a sparkle of diamonds on the snow. The large burr oak standing to the left of the barn lifts its crusted branches into the dark.

My breaths dissolve in the cold air, and suddenly everything is beautiful. I'm free and it's beautiful here. And in a few minutes I'll be warm under the covers with my wife. What could be better than this? Everyone should have this simple peace, not broken even by the crunch of my footsteps leading to the car.

But there's no sleep that night. How could I have been such a thoughtless fool? Why didn't I ask just to be sure? We could have talked. I've never been to Detroit.

In a sudden surge of craziness I slip out of bed and get dressed, careful not to wake my wife. I need to know more. In a few minutes I find myself standing in the road leading to Julian's house. My footprint trail to the house is clear, a single set leading up the path to the front door. And I see the return set of my prints leading to the spot where my car was parked. But there is no light on in the house. It seems abandoned, solitary, with its upper windows looking down on the procession of snow-covered fence posts trudging toward the woods. And there are no other footprints leading away from the house.

So he's in there still, crouching against the coal bin wall, and I know he's waiting to make his next move, knowing it's impossible to hide in some Alabama barn.

✗

Emilio DeGrazia, a long-time resident of Winona, Minnesota, founded *Great River Review* in 1977. A collection of fiction, *Enemy Country,* was selected by Anne Tyler for a Writer's Choice Award, and a novel, *Billy Brazil,* won a Minnesota Voices award. A second collection, *Seventeen Grams of Soul,* received a Minnesota Book Award. He has also published two collections of essays and two of poetry, including most recently *What Trees Know.*

OUT OF A FOG

BARB GOFFMAN

My boyfriend dumped me a week before Thanksgiving. It felt like a Mack truck slammed into me, and after I skidded across the pavement, leaving behind torn flesh and what remained of my heart, it kept on coming, rolling right over me. First the front tires, huge and heavy, their treads filled with razor-sharp pebbles. Then the back ones, too, ensuring I was good and flattened.

"It's not you," he said. "It's me." That old cliché.

We were sitting on my bed. A light snow was falling outside—unusual for November in Ann Arbor. But then, nothing was normal that night. The swirling flakes seemed to dance in the glow of a nearby streetlamp, taunting me with their joy.

"I don't understand." My voice quivered. "You love me. I know you do."

Three years we'd been together. Since we met in Econ freshman year. We'd talked about the future. About forever.

"I can't spend Thanksgiving with your family next week knowing this isn't going to work," he said.

"But it is working. We're happy."

"No, we're not—I'm not."

My eyes watered, and he jumped off the bed, as if my tears might sting him or, even worse, make him change his mind. He tried to pace but could barely take a dozen steps before hitting one wall or another. We'd always appreciated the coziness of my bedroom. But now he looked trapped. A feral cat desperate to escape his cage.

"Let's not do this," he said. "Just accept it's over."

"No." I rose. "I don't accept it. Just last night you told me for the millionth time you love me. We made love. Right here. How could you do this now?" And then I knew. "There's someone else, isn't there?"

"No." He sounded wounded, as if the accusation was unthinkable. As if he were the one being dumped.

"Then why are you doing this?"

He sighed. "Two weeks ago I woke up, as if coming out of a fog." He nodded at the bed. "I looked at you and thought, 'What am I doing? I don't love her.'"

My thigh began shaking, and I had to grab it to stop the spasm.

"So you've been faking it since then?" My words got louder, one by one, until I was screaming. "Every kiss, every endearment has been a lie?"

"I've been trying to recapture what we had." He grabbed my hands and gave me a sad smile. "You're so great. I know you'll find someone else."

Then a look of pity settled on his face. Pity!

I wrenched my hands from his and ordered him out. After slamming the apartment door shut, I whirled around, desperate to inflict some pain of my own. I grabbed a framed photo of us, all moony-eyed smiles last New Year's Eve, and I smashed it against my desk. The glass shattered, the splintered pieces flying. A metaphor for my heart. And my life.

* * * *

The next few weeks passed in a daze. I kept trying to figure out how he could love me one minute and not love me the next.

Nothing made any sense until early December. I was walking to the library to study. I'd needed to get away from my neighbor who kept blasting Christmas songs. Between the breakup, finals, and the relentless cheer coming through the thin walls, destroying her stereo was the only thing that would have made me holly jolly that day. That's when I saw him kissing some blonde with long straight hair.

My breath caught. It hadn't even been three weeks since our breakup. How could he be kissing someone else? How could he have moved on so quickly?

And I realized … he *had* cheated on me. He must have.

I shook as the enormity of his lies and betrayal washed over me.

With rage boiling inside, I vowed he would pay.

* * * *

Over winter break I bought myself a folding knife for Christmas. Easy to open. Easy to hide in my coat pocket. When classes resumed in January I followed him around, getting to know his new schedule. Where he went. When he was alone.

When he was vulnerable.

Not having a boyfriend anymore, I had a lot of free time on my hands.

I couldn't bear knowing he was out there, happy with someone else. Smiling at her. Kissing her. Loving her. So I planned to kill him on Valentine's Day—the day that mocks people like me, who have been dropped like stinking garbage. I'd do it right after midnight as the evil day began. That's when he'd leave the undergrad library, where he worked three nights a week.

When the witching hour finally approached, I perched on a cold stone bench outside the library, wearing a new hat that hid my hair and forehead and a scarf that covered my mouth. I was eyes and a nose. Unrecognizable. Ready to give the bastard exactly what he deserved.

But I hadn't planned on the blonde showing up, walking toward the library.

Damn it. She was going to ruin my plans. … Or maybe—I smiled—*she could fit into them.*

Then a girl left the library and approached Blondie, not three yards from me.

"You have good V Day plans?" the friend asked.

"We're supposed to go to the Gandy Dancer." A fancy restaurant. Pricey, especially for students. He took me there last Valentine's Day.

"Supposed to?" the friend asked.

Blondie shrugged.

Her friend's mouth dropped open. "You're not—"

"I'm just not feeling it anymore."

"You're going to break up with him now? Tomorrow's Valentine's Day."

"Exactly. I can't bear going through this romantic dinner. He stares at me like he's a puppy. It's pathetic." Blondie nodded at the door. "Here he comes."

As her friend scurried away, calling, "I'll want details," I watched him. He was carrying a red rose and wearing—she was right—a puppy-dog expression.

I blinked repeatedly. He'd never looked at me like that.

Why had he never looked at me like that?

Had he never loved me at all?

The clarity came sharp as a slap across the cheek. He hadn't.

But he sure seemed to love her.

She took the rose and they walked off. And as if coming out of a fog, I followed them, easing the knife from my pocket when we entered a dim part of the path.

Suddenly they stopped short and he cried, "No!"

I recognized that tone. That despair.

And I grinned.

I raised my arm … and tossed the knife into a trash can.

It was the perfect punishment. He was going to hurt, just like me.

Barb Goffman won the 2020 Readers Award given out by *Ellery Queen's Mystery Magazine* for her story "Dear Emily Etiquette." She's also won the Agatha, Macavity, and Silver Falchion awards and has been nominated for major crime-writing awards thirty-three times. In addition to *EQMM* and *Black Cat Mystery Magazine*, her stories have appeared in *Alfred Hitchcock's Mystery Magazine* and many anthologies. She works as a freelance editor, focusing on cozy and traditional mysteries. www.barbgoffman.com

EL PESCADOR ZURDO

(THE LEFT-HANDED FISHERMAN)

TOM LARSEN

Captain Ernesto Guillén despised the heat. Carrying nearly one hundred eighty pounds on his five-feet-six-inch frame meant that a day spent in the heat and humidity of the tiny Ecuadorian fishing village of Manglaralto was a day of misery, sweat, itching and chafing.

Adding to the humiliation was his tiny office, shoehorned into a corner of the windowless concrete bunker that was the *Unidad Policía Comunidad* building along the E-15 highway outside of town. How Guillén missed his cool and airy office back in Cuenca. Everyone who knew him said it was his fault, and he couldn't disagree. He had been banished to this coastal backwater after thirty-five years of service in the National Police, not for soliciting bribes, manufacturing evidence, or having sex with one of his subordinates. He had done all of that and more, but it had all been overlooked. It could have been due to the astonishing rate at which he solved crimes, or the damaging material that he had collected on his superiors over time.

Whatever it was, he had finally committed the one transgression that could not be overlooked—publicly embarrassing a prominent *Cuencano* businessman and political supporter of the mayor himself.

Guillén focused his anger this morning on the man sitting across the desk from him. He had already decided that this man, a suspect in a brutal murder, was innocent, but he continued glaring at him, nonetheless. It amused him to see this man, a strapping fisherman with arms and legs roped with muscle and skin burnt nearly black from years at sea, cowering before him.

"You have to believe me," the man whined, his calloused hands out in front of him in a pleading gesture.

Guillén merely stared back at him, saying nothing, his dark eyes boring into the man from beneath a prominent forehead and a pair of bushy eyebrows that could be mistaken for black caterpillars.

The sound of shrill angry voices and blaring car horns attracted their attention. Sergeant Baltra rushed in through the front door of the station, followed so closely by a young female *patrullera* that she nearly collided with him when he skidded to a halt in front of Guillén's desk.

"What's going on out there, Sergeant?" the captain demanded.

The sergeant, despite his youth and general appearance of fitness and having run no more than ten meters, struggled mightily trying to catch his breath—so mightily in fact that the young *patrullera* spoke for him.

"There is a big group of villagers gathering out front, sir."

"What do they want?"

"Him, Sir." The sergeant, having regained his wind, pointed at the fisherman sitting across from Guillén, causing the man's head to snap up and his eyes to widen.

"Ah," said Guillén. "Vigilante justice, right?"

"Yes, sir. What should we do?"

"Tell them to go away. Tell them this isn't the killer." Guillén waved off-handedly in the direction of the erstwhile suspect. The fisherman's eyes widened even farther, and his mouth snapped open like a *corvina* rising to the bait.

"He's not?" Sergeant Baltra and the policewoman spoke nearly as one.

"No, he's not. Now, go tell them!"

"Me?" Baltra said. "Shouldn't you tell them? You're the captain."

Guillén leaned back in his chair, lacing his fingers across his swollen stomach. "Do you want to be a sergeant all your life, Baltra?"

"Well, I … I …"

The captain sighed noisily and got up from his chair. The short exchange with Baltra confirmed everything that he had long suspected about the man. Like the majority of policemen in Ecuador, Baltra came from humble beginnings. It was quite enough for men like him to have a job that afforded them a steady paycheck, a certain amount of authority and the chance to strut about in his starched, tight-fitting uniform. It was surprising to Guillén that the man even had what it took to make sergeant, but that was as far as he would ever go.

"Stay here and keep this man company," he told the sergeant, indicating the fisherman, who still appeared as if someone had shocked him with a cattle prod. He motioned to the young policewoman to follow him. She never even glanced toward the crestfallen Baltra, her immediate supervisor. *This one will go far,* Guillén thought. As they approached the door, he saw her unfasten the strap on her service revolver.

"No, no," he cautioned. "No need for that. As a matter of fact.…" He reached beneath his suit jacket and removed his service weapon. "Let's just leave the guns inside."

With only a split second of hesitation, the *patrullera* followed his lead and placed her revolver on the counter, next to his Glock. She turned and went through the door, allowing the captain to admire the tight fit of her uniform as she went. So many of the female officers tried to hide their femininity, something that Guillén would never understand. This one, while she didn't flaunt it, certainly had to know the effect she had on men and used it to her advantage.

"Baltra!" Guillén barked as he left the building. "Secure those weapons and lock the door behind us."

Officer Ruíz hesitated once she got a good look at the assembled crowd, about twenty men and half a dozen women. They pushed against the tall chain-link gate with renewed ferocity once they saw they had an audience. Guillén moved toward them at a steady pace, feeling for a moment like the youthful gung-ho officer that he once was, not the bloated gasbag he had become. Ruíz trailed in his wake.

The mob wasn't armed, but Guillén knew that could change in an instant. If things went sideways, rocks, pieces of metal, and tree branches would be quickly gathered up and used as weapons. As he approached the front gate, the captain absent-mindedly rubbed his fingers along his right side. Through his shirt, now soaked with sweat, he could feel the outline of the thick scar where he had been hit by a sharpened piece of bamboo wielded by a *Shuar* tribesman during the indigenous group's ten-day occupation of the government offices in Cuenca in 1999.

The front courtyard of the police station was a gravel pad, littered with motorcycles, bicycles and a few cars and pickups that had been confiscated because the owners had been guilty of the crime of not having enough cash on hand to bribe their way out of one traffic mishap or another. Guillén walked steadily forward, and the crowd became more subdued with every step he took in their direction. He felt energized. Maybe when word got back to Cuenca, this would be the case that made them come to him, hats in hands, begging him to return. In less capable hands—Baltra's, for example—the mob would have already broken through or climbed over the gate, gathered up random bike parts and beaten the poor slob inside to death.

Guillén recognized the man who appeared to be in charge of the group, although he couldn't think of his name. The man wore gray dress pants and a dark blue button-down shirt, in contrast to the stained and tattered workmen's clothing that was the uniform for the rest of the group.

"Tell your people it's time to go home," Guillén said through the gate, standing inches from the leader on the other side. In his peripheral vision he saw Ruíz fidgeting nervously, her hand continually going to her holster. When she remembered that she had surrendered her gun, her hand jerked back as if she had burned it.

"We only want justice, *Capitán*," the leader said.

"And, you'll have it. You have my word on that. But—"

"Your word?" The group leader spread his hands and looked around him as if to say; *can you believe this guy?* The crowd began murmuring, but before they got out of control, he cut them off with a slight raise of his hand. "Your word, a policeman's word," he said, locking eyes with the captain, "means nothing to us. I would suggest that you turn this man over to us, and we will see that he is punished for what he has done."

"Who are you?" Guillén asked, his tone showing the man respect but making it clear who was in charge.

"My name is Gustavo Astudillo. I am the president of the local fisherman's union.

"So then, this man, this Cepeda ...." Guillén hooked a thumb over his shoulder in the direction of the police station. "He's one of yours. No?"

Astudillo turned to one side and spat on the ground. "No, *Capitán.* He is not one of us." Those close enough to hear him murmured their agreement. *"¡Èl es Peruano!"*

Peruvian? Guillén was surprised. There was a longstanding animosity between Ecuadorians and Peruvians, dating back hundreds of years, to the point where most people on either side weren't sure why. *Maybe I should let them have him,* he thought. But then he remembered the recent incident in a small border town where a group much like this one had pulled from the police station a couple of men suspected of kidnapping a young girl. They beat the men and burned them to death, only to find that they had the wrong men. *Not on my watch!* The captain growled under his breath.

"Señor Astudillo," Guillén said in a low voice. "Cepeda did not kill the young man."

"Of course, he did!" Astudillo responded. "He was seen on the beach that night."

Guillén turned to the man standing to Astudillo's left. "Show me your hands," he demanded.

The fisherman, barefoot and wearing only a pair of stained jogging shorts and a sun-bleached knock-off LA Lakers jersey, hesitated for a moment but then did as he was told. Guillén motioned for him to extend his hands palms up, close to the fence.

"See there?" The captain pointed to a series of thin scars and one fresh cut on the man's left palm. "You hold your knife in your right hand, when you fillet the fish, or cut bait, or whatever else you need to do. Correct?" The man nodded, and Guillén saw the realization begin to dawn on Astudillo's face.

"You, my friend, are right-handed. Yes?" Without waiting for a response, Guillén turned and pointed back toward the police station with a dramatic flourish. "As is Señor Cepeda!"

The fisherman stood and stared at his outstretched hands as if unsure what to do with them. Astudillo's face contorted and then relaxed. He nodded his head slowly, as if in agreement with something.

"The killer was ... is left-handed?" he said, to no one in particular.

"That's right," Guillén said. He stood for a moment, watching as this bit of information worked its way through the crowd like a breeze through a field of pampas grass. Then he removed the padlock from the gate and pulled it open.

"Baltra!" he yelled over his shoulder. "Put on some coffee for these folks. Use the big *cafetera,* the one we used for the governor's visit a few weeks ago.

"Ruíz," he said, fishing in his wallet and handing her a small sheaf of bills. "Go to that *panadería* on *Calle Diez de Agosto* and get some sweetbreads and some juice. Some plastic cups and some napkins. And check with Baltra. Make sure there's enough sugar and milk."

Ruíz looked as if she might object, but Guillén stared her down. She was smart and pretty and he was sure she had the makings of a good cop, but right now, he was in charge. Anyone under his command, man or woman, would damn well follow his orders without hesitation or discussion.

* * * *

The formerly angry mob of villagers now milled around the police station as if enjoying an unexpected fiesta day. They slurped coffee and juice and attacked the sack of sweet treats that Ruíz had brought, leaving hardly a crumb for the seabirds that had gathered overhead in anticipation. They gawked at the pictures and posters on the walls, and at one point someone opened a door, revealing a group of night-shift patrolmen playing cards in their underwear. The men in the crowd laughed and pointed while the women either hooted and whistled or giggled behind their hands. Guillén stood by and observed the carnival-like scene with a slight smile on his face.

"Congratulations, Captain." Gustavo Astudillo saluted him with his coffee cup. "You handled the situation quite well."

"Who organized this 'situation' as you call it?" Guillén asked.

"Organized? Well, I'm not quite sure. It just happened; you know." Astudillo reached out to touch the captain's forearm. He lowered his voice to barely above a whisper. "You're not from here, are you, captain?"

"No, I'm not."

"Well, the people here … they don't trust the police. And, with good reason. You … they … strut around here in their starched uniforms and spit-shined shoes, like they're gods. They disrespect our women, take our fish and our produce without paying. They set up bogus traffic stops but they never write a ticket. If you don't have enough cash to pay them off…." Astudillo swept his arm in a wide arc, taking in the rows of rusting bikes and motorcycles that littered the yard.

"We're dealing with a murder here," Guillén reminded him. "Not some traffic infraction."

"Exactly!" Astudillo spit on the ground again. "You investigate nothing. Robberies, assaults, now murder." He spat the words out as he ticked them off on his fingers.

Guillén reached out and grabbed the man's hand.

"I see that you are left-handed, Señor Astudillo."

"So what?" The union president yanked his hand from the captain's grasp. "Surely, you don't suspect me?"

"Not at all, not at all. But—" Guillén paused as if a thought had just occurred to him. "Did you know that less than ten percent of the world's population is left-handed?"

"So?" Astudillo's brows creased in suspicion.

"How many citizens live in the village of Manglaralto?"

"About a thousand, I think."

"And for our purposes, we can assume half of them are men. So, five hundred?"

Astudillo nodded in confirmation, frowning as he waited for the trick that he assumed was coming.

"And, at least half of them are too young or too old to have committed this crime. So that leaves about two hundred fifty. Right?"

Astudillo shrugged "You're the detective."

"Yes," Guillén agreed. "I am. This young man who was murdered was nearly five-feet-ten-inches tall, much taller than you or I or most of the men in this room. Yet he was killed by a single blow to the back of his head. The left side of his head. With the pointed corner of a two-kilogram lead fishing weight."

"Then just about every man in town is a suspect. This is a fishing village, Captain."

"Yes, it is!" Guillén agreed. "But, if we complete our little math exercise, we find that only about twenty-five of these fishermen would likely be left-handed. And we've already eliminated you." He leaned closer and whispered, "It wasn't you, was it?"

"Of course not. Look, Captain. I have a job to get back to."

"A job that's more important than finding who killed this fine young man? Tsk, tsk. Señor Astudillo. You know...." Guillén rubbed his chin, mimicking deep thought. "Who better to identify these twenty-four suspects than the illustrious president of the fishermen's union?"

He placed a hand on the man's shoulder, gently but with purpose, and steered him into the building.

* * * *

Guillén heaved his bulk into his battered old office chair, causing it to squeal in protest. Across from him sat Gustavo Astudillo, frowning mightily to show that he had more important places to be, and Officer Ruíz, with her notebook open on the desk in front of her.

Guillén had sent Sergeant Baltra to take Cepeda home, with an admonition loud enough for the entire group to hear. "If any harm comes to this man, you will all have to answer to me!"

* * * *

"This young man who was murdered?" Guillén consulted the single sheet of paper in front of him. "Gilberto Vasquez. Eighteen years of age. He was very popular in town. No?"

"Yes, he was." Astudillo looked down at his hands as he spoke. "His father was lost at sea when he was no more than five or six. His mother...." Astudillo shrugged and spread his hands. "She went crazy, drinking, neglecting the child. His *abuelitos* took him in and his mother finally left town. Guayaquil, I hear, but no one knows for sure."

"It must have been difficult for his grandparents," Ruíz said softly, with just the right amount of sympathy, the perfect counterpoint to Guillén's gruffness.

"It was. Of course, it was," Astudillo agreed. "But we all pitched in; made sure they had enough food, bought him toys and clothing, his school uniforms and books. He graduated this year and is headed to university in the fall." Astudillo sat a little straighter. "That's the kind of town this is!"

"It's also the kind of town where this wonderful young man you speak of was brutally bludgeoned and left to die on the beach," Guillén said, and watched with satisfaction as Astudillo's shoulders slumped.

"But here's what's interesting," the captain went on. "Someone went to a lot of trouble to hide the body. There's evidence that the boy had been in the water for sixteen hours, maybe more. So, someone either took him out in a boat, or maybe just let the tide do its work. But...." He peered at the union chief, who looked away. "When the tide came in this morning, at five twenty-seven, by the way, it tossed the young man's body onto the rocks not five hundred meters south of where the fishing fleet gathers. Don't you find that odd? I do."

When Astudillo said nothing, Guillén switched gears. "What does the president of the fisherman's union do? I noticed when I took your hand earlier that you have a lot of faded scarring, but nothing recent."

Astudillo looked down at his hands as if trying to verify the truth of what the captain had said. "I negotiate deals with fish-processing companies and the big canneries. I make sure that our people get the best prices possible, I also—"

"But you were a fisherman, yes?"

"Of course. For nearly twenty years I went out every day. Sun, rain, wind. It didn't matter."

"Then, you are familiar with the tides in this area?"

"This is our livelihood, Captain. We learn the tides from our fathers and grandfathers."

Ruíz got up and stood in front of the large wall map that was mounted behind the captain's desk.

"The young man ...Vásquez," she said, "his body was found right about here." She marked the spot with a slender forefinger.

"Yes, that's right. You see...." Astudillo stood and joined her at the map. "Just a few meters south of there. Right here, where the river, *Río Atravesado* it's called.... This time of year, the rainy season, the flow is so high that it affects the tides. You know—"

"And you know this," the captain interrupted, "because you've lived here all your life. And, you were a fisherman."

"Yes. Exactly! That's why we suspected Cepeda. He's only been here less than a year. Not even a full season."

"No. Not exactly. I think you wanted it to be Cepeda, because he's a *Peruano.* But he's also an experienced fisherman. He told me earlier that he fished at home in Perú for fifteen years. He only moved here because he married an *Ecuatoriana.* He knows as much about tides as you or anyone else in this town, Señor Astudillo. As a matter of fact, do you know what he told me?"

"No. How would I?" Astudillo sat down and Guillén took his place at the wall map.

"He told me," Guillén said, stabbing at the map with a huge sausage-like finger, "that this was probably the very worst spot in the area to dump something if you didn't want it to be found."

"Like a body?" Astudillo snorted. "It figures he would know about that. Wouldn't it?"

"I see that you aren't ready quite yet to give up on your little attempt to put Cepeda in the box," Guillén said, sitting back at his desk. "But, you should. Because it's keeping you from seeing my point."

"What is your point, captain?" Clearly frustrated, Astudillo began to stand up, but a look from Guillén drove him back into his chair as surely as if he had been punched.

"The captain's point is," Ruíz said, still standing in front of the wall map, "that the killer is not a fisherman."

"Not a fisherman?" Now Astudillo did stand up. "This whole town … we're all fisherman." He waved his arm to take in the few stragglers that remained from the morning's protest.

"Sit down!" Guillén said and the union president did so quickly.

"Of course, not everyone in town is a fisherman, Señor Astudillo. I'm not a fisherman, for example. Officer Ruíz. Does she look like a fisherman?"

"No. I suppose you're right. But—"

"I, myself? I think it's somebody wealthy, prominent in the community. A banker maybe? A priest? No. They take a vow of poverty or something. Don't they?"

Officer Ruíz's cell phone pinged, notifying her of a text message. She read it and handed the phone to Captain Guillén. He studied the message on the screen for a long time, his big thick tongue protruding from the corner of his mouth as he concentrated.

"What is your relationship with Hermann Vanger, Señor Astudillo?" Guillén placed the phone faceup on his desk.

"Why are you asking me this? What does it have to do with anything?" Astudillo's response was weak, barely audible.

"You know very well why I'm asking," the captain said, his voice low but menacing. "Of course, I already know the answer, but let's pretend I don't. Who is Hermann Vanger?" He leaned forward and his gaze bored into Astudillo.

"Hermann Vanger is the coastal representative for Schweiger Seafoods. It's a German concern."

"And one of your biggest clients."

"Yes." With each answer Astudillo seemed to withdraw further into himself.

"And, it seems that Herr Vanger has a daughter. He glanced down at the phone. "Anneka. Sixteen, I believe."

"I think so, yes."

"And Vanger has been less than enamored of her new boyfriend, even though everyone else in town thinks so highly of him. I'm talking of course about Gilberto Vásquez.

"I wonder," Guillén continued, as if talking to himself, "will Herr Vanger turn out to be left-handed? What do you think, Señor Astudillo?"

"I want an attorney."

Guillén nodded in agreement. "That is probably a very good idea. I imagine a man like Hermann Vanger will have a very good one. Perhaps he will let him represent you as well." Guillén paused. "After all that you've done for him.

"But, now that I think about it for a moment, it really would be in your best interest to distance yourself from him right now. We know what happened." He indicated Officer Ruíz, who appeared delighted to be included along with the great crime-solver. "Vanger encountered young Gilberto on the beach that night … either by chance or by design. Doesn't matter. They argued, things got out of hand and Vanger picked up a fishing weight and killed him. Simple as that. He's German, no? So, I assume he's taller than most Ecuadorians.

"Then, realizing what he'd done, he first tried, clumsily it seems, to cover up his crime. Then, what did he do?" Guillén looked around as if the answer might be somewhere in the room. "I'll tell you what he did. He called his old friend, the president of the fishermen's union.

"And you were more than happy to help. You implicated the *Peruano*, and because you knew that sooner or later we would find that he wasn't the one, you organized this mob to ensure that he would never go to trial."

In the ensuing silence, as if on cue, Guillén's stomach grumbled like thunder before a storm. Astudillo and Ruíz tried to act as if they hadn't heard. The captain stood up and came around the desk, leaning down so that his face was inches away from the suspect's.

"As you can probably tell," he said, "I'm a man who likes his food." He glanced at his wristwatch. "Now it's past three o'clock and I've had no lunch. So, let's get this over with here and now. Was anything I just said untrue?"

Astudillo shook his head slightly.

"It happened exactly as I said?"

Astudillo nodded.

"Say it!"

"Yes," Astudillo said softly. "It happened like you said." He buried his face in his hands and began to weep.

Guillén stood for a moment, regarding the man with disgust. Then his stomach rumbled again, and he turned away.

"Take his statement," he told Officer Ruíz. "I'll get some men to round up Vanger and I'll be back once I've taken care of this." He patted his massive stomach with affection.

As he turned to leave, Astudillo laid a hand on his forearm.

"Can we talk in private, you and I?" he said, nodding in the direction of Officer Ruíz who had already taken a seat at the captain's desk and was rifling through the drawers looking for the correct form to take the man's statement. She looked up at the captain, a question on her face.

"Stay where you are." Guillén held his hand out. He brushed Astudillo's hand from his arm. "You have probably heard some things about me. I know how you small town folks gossip like a bunch of old women. A lot of it is true, but I have never in my life allowed the likes of you to get away with murder."

* * * *

As he left the building, the captain saw Sergeant Baltra deep in conversation with a couple of fishermen over by the impound yard. Money surreptitiously changed hands and the two left astride a pair of Kawasaki 125s, their engines smoking from disuse but running, nonetheless. Sergeant Baltra watched them go, stuffing the wad of bills into his pocket.

I'll be damned, Guillén thought. *Maybe there's hope for the sergeant yet.*

Tom Larsen was born and raised in New Jersey and was awarded a degree in Civil Engineering from Rutgers University. Tom is the author of six novels in the crime genre, all available on Amazon: http://www.amazon.com/TOM-LARSEN/e/ B00N00JLZM. Tom's short fiction has been published in *Alfred Hitchcock's Mystery Magazine, Mystery Tribune,* and *Black Cat Mystery Magazine.* He is the 2020 recipient of the *Black Orchid Novella Award,* presented by the Nero Wolfe Society.

A BLUE UMBRELLA SKY

R.S. MORGAN

Sheriff Wayne was giving me a ride out of our nowhere Kentucky town, a week after my mother's fiery death, when we saw *that* bumper sticker. "I saw *that*," the bumper sticker read. There was also a five-letter word in a smaller font at the bottom of the bumper sticker we couldn't make out. So, stuck at the Walmart red light and Wayne and I being curious types, he inched his police SUV closer.

Wayne's also my fiancé. Been going together for ten years, since junior year in high school. Would have probably been married for nine years if not for one problem: I couldn't stay in town and he couldn't leave. Our love story, however, didn't begin like a Taylor Swift song of a high school romance. He wasn't the star quarterback. He was a so-so lineman. Big, the biggest boy on the team: six feet five inches and an etched two hundred seventy. But slow moving. Slow talking, too. But not slow in the head. Also, except for the teacup ears, kind of cute. I also liked his kind smile, which, yeah, took a while to set up. And while schoolboy Wayne was something less than the star quarterback, schoolgirl me was a whole lot more than the captain of the cheerleaders. I was the halftime entertainment.

The five-letter word was karma. Wayne and I locked eyes as an eerie chill ran through me. Karma's more than a word to me. I've dedicated my life to creating good karma. I even have a red lotus flower, the karma flower, tattooed on the back of my neck. Wayne's slow smile set up as the light turned green. Wayne stayed put. Kept his eyes on me and put his Explorer in park and lit up his rooftop panic lights. Wayne was loose. I was wound semi-tight. Somehow it worked.

"Yeah, Allison, karma sure saw what you did to your daddy's girlfriend and, oh boy, old girl karma must have had a fine belly laugh."

Wayne and most others had loved the public embarrassment I had laid on Rebecca. I had not and I did not return his smile. Men. Don't they understand anything? I was still in a daze and in no mood for smiles or laughter. My mother's too soon and too senseless death was the reason for most of my bewilderment. Yet I was also still rattled about what I had done to Rebecca. I had never snapped. Never been violent. Never, I suppose, gone insane.

His smile turned into a chuckle as the bloated pickups and SUVs behind us politely merged into the right-hand lane. I nodded at his happy yet clueless face then pulled my backpack and hula hoops from the backseat and hopped out and walked up to the karma car, which was a tiny Toyota sedan, a style of vehicle almost extinct around here.

I opened the passenger's door and squeezed in with my gear. The driver was an old Kentucky hippie, his silver hair in a ponytail. He didn't look stoned or nervous. But he sure did look surprised to see me in his front seat. Most likely, he knew who I was: the local girl who was almost famous.

"You're free to go," I calmly said as Wayne's spinning red and blue lights washed over us. "Now please take me to Parts Unknown."

* * * *

"I've known your mom since kindergarten. She was even my BFF for a year." Rebecca said to me the night before I left for Parts Unknown. "And your mom and dad had a wonderful marriage for many years. But people grow apart and adultery happens. If she hadn't died, your dad was going to divorce her."

Because of you, I thought but did not say.

Yet I tried not to judge either her or my father, thought about *my* BFF from high school. Over a bottle of Pinot last summer, she told tight-lipped me about her torrid affair. "Yeah, there's guilt," she said. "But there's also an upside." Then she smiled a sly and secret smile. I laughed. Understood. But my father and maneater Rebecca?

Rebecca was the other local girl who had become almost famous. She'd been a year behind my dad in high school so they'd also known each other forever. Yet in the way a wad of gum knows the bottom of a shoe. My dad being Mr. Sticky.

Rebecca anchored Eyewitness News in Louisville for twenty years and my dad worshipped her on his flat screen each night. Some say she was kicked to the curb for the usual reason: a fresh beauty agreed to read the teleprompter for a third of Rebecca's salary. Most, however, say she was fired for being a total bitch once too often, her termination nastiness taking place at a Halloween fundraiser when she made a witch cry.

We were on my father's porch, in white wicker chairs, face-to-face, knees almost touching, drinking sweet iced tea, as dusk and a gorgeous autumn evening began to roll up from the folds and creases. We had one of the highest and nicest houses in our part of the Cumberland Gap. Nerdy dad, a CPA, had done well. Well enough to have his high-school goddess, thirty years after graduation, on his porch.

The cicadas begin to chirp. The butterfly wind chimes whispered sweetly. The lavender candles on the tables beside our chairs scented the pink horizon. I was there to apologize for the epic humiliation I had laid on her at my mom's funeral breakfast and to thank her for not pressing charges.

I calmly stared at her. Took note of the lip and hair issues I had caused. She stared back, smug and snotty, as she waited for me to grovel. At forty-six, she still had that cute chipmunk face. Still had those soft curves on a hard body. Had the technical end down, too. Right down to the glow-in-the-dark whiteness of her teeth and the state-of-the-art plastic on her chest. She looked great. Yet manufactured. Really, Dad, this is your type of woman? She reminded me of a middle-aged Barbie and when she wore something that clung to her like shrink wrap, which was all the time she was around my dad, I could just about see the model number stamped on her behind. And while she looked and acted as fake as Barbie around my dad, she kept it real around me.

My mom, who was both a natural woman and my best friend, lost her life when one of our many lost boys coming down from his Cadillac high fell asleep at the wheel and crossed the double yellow. I was on tour in Tennessee when I got the call, and after a good cry in the arms of Clarissa, my starry-eyed under-study, I numbly drove back to Middlesboro to bury my mom. Then to deal with her abrupt and painful death and also find out my father was having an affair with a diabolical doll, yeah, that was too much for me to process and mellow me flipped out.

Maybe it was the vodka, which I smelled on her breath, that was giving her courage to be alone with me. Wished she had offered me some to pour into my tea. Rebecca tilted her head. Probably wondering when—or if—I was going to speak. I remained silent as I continued to stare at her with a Zen-like blankness.

"Your dad and I reconnected at last year's high-school reunion," she said, in her crisp television voice. "It was love at first sight, thirty years later, for me."

Love at first sight with his money, I thought as I continued with my unblinking silence.

"This is the part, Allison, where you're supposed to stop being a spoiled brat and be happy for your father." Rebecca paused and took a long gulp of her spiked tea. "No? You don't want to talk this out? Then let me explain the situation another way. Some years back, a good friend accused me of making love to her husband. Ask me, 'And what did you say to that?' It's a good reply. Maybe my best."

Instead of asking, I zoned out on her mask of a face. Wondered how long she took to put on her makeup. I wear elaborate mascaras and shadows for cat eyes when I perform, but offstage, like my mom, I'm a natural woman. Natural and exotic looking, at least for small-town Kentucky. My mother, whom I resemble, was Lebanese—a stone-cold Arabian beauty—and I get the occasional fisheye from visitors from other small towns because of my wavy black hair and sharp features. Wayne says I look like Princess Jasmine.

Rebecca leaned in, almost nose to nose, and dropped her voice to a whisper. "I said, 'I wouldn't exactly call it making love.'" Was I supposed to gasp at her snarky betrayal? I held onto my poker face. Waited for the take-away message. As expected, it was a short wait. Nor was I surprised when her whisper morphed into a witchy hiss. "What I'm trying to say, what you have to accept, daddy's little precious, is that I know what men want, I know how to get my way with men, and your father is caught in my web."

The wind chimes played their melodies. I remained nose-to-nose and mute. Her subtle perfume drifted. Was she trying to provoke me into round two of our cat fight? Didn't know, didn't care. I just wanted her to confirm something I already knew. Eventually she relaxed. Leaned back and melted into the high woven back of her white chair. Basked in the good fortune that led to her spinning her web at the right time and place.

Eventually I spoke.

"Do you plan on marrying my father?"

"I do."

Cute. Also no surprise. After that she'd pillow talk my dad into changing his will. Then she'd try to screw him to death. All of that was bad.

Then it got worse. Violently and mysteriously worse.

* * * *

Back at Parts Unknown, which is the name of the one-ring circus I headline, I let it all out with Clarissa. Clarissa is more than my understudy; she's the little sister I never had. And, boy, did I unload on little sister. I vented about the gold digger my dad was going to marry, Dad's two million dollars I always believed would be mine someday, and my bad karma meltdown.

At my mom's wake, Rebecca acted as my dad's official greeter. At the church service, she sat next to my dad, with me on the other side. Same deal at the funeral breakfast. And while I didn't know my dad was cheating on my mom, the rest of Middlesboro's big shots sure did. Yet to have their coming-out party at my mom's funeral? Absolutely shameless. Despite all that, I believed I was handling everything quite well. Stunned about my mom's death. Gobsmacked about my dad's too-soon and too-evil girlfriend. Still, I had no plans to misbehave.

I was going to go with the flow like the rest of the town and act like my mom never existed, even though we had just buried her an hour ago. In a way, my mom never had existed. She had lived an invisible life, happy to stay in the background and be my dad's wife and my soulmate. She was such a ghost she never said anything to me, or probably anyone, about Rebecca. Just took it.

My plan was to also be a ghost. Just take it. What changed those plans? Perhaps it was the predatory look Rebecca shot at my father and then at me. As if we were two oblivious flies caught in her web. Perhaps it was the slender, spidery fingers she arched on Dad's thigh. But, most likely, it was because my mom was good, Rebecca was awful, and I could no longer tolerate awful replacing good.

One second I was a ghost, sipping tomato juice. The next I was all flesh and blood and fury and my wrathful hand was twisted in Rebecca's yellow nylon hair. I yanked her out of her chair and flung her. She staggered on her stilettos, back and forth then side to side, like a wrestler hamming it up, then thumped down on her butt on the dance floor and with the mayor and the chief of police looking on and the dance floor looking like a wrestling ring, I pointed a trembling clump of her dark-rooted hair at her startled face and spread-eagle legs and screamed words I had never previously said, "Stay away from my father or I'll rip off your face!"

The cell phones were out by now, of course, videoing as Rebecca scrambled to her feet, and by the hot look on her face and the way her acrylic nails were curled and set to slice, she was ready for WWF-worthy action. I'm certain almost all would have loved to see us catfight: the daughter of the widower versus the girlfriend of the widower, both pretty, both icons in their nowhere town, both dressed in dressed-to-kill little black funeral dresses. Some stood up with their phones to get a better angle, ready for the scratching and shrieking to commence.

Fortunately, my giant fiancé, who had been at the buffet table brownnosing his boss, bear-hugged me from behind, and while I kicked at Rebecca and sent a mule flying that caught her in the mouth, he carried me outside and, before driving me away, he let me pound out my hyperventilating craziness on his chest.

* * * *

"You're kinda strange," a middle-school wise girl once told me at her Boys and Girls Club, where I do an outreach program. At each show stop, I give youngsters "the talk": study hard, eat mostly fruits and vegetables, exercise often, stay away from drugs, don't live your life on your phone, live a life of good karma. Then, modestly dressed in a tracksuit, I do the PG version of my hula hoop act.

I smiled at the wise girl as her posse laughed. I am kinda strange. A grown woman who is still passionate about hula hoops has to be peculiar. There's no laughter, however, when I cue my electronica music and step into my first hoop and shimmy it up. And there's just silence when I raise my leg above my head and spin a hoop on an ankle. My act flows from there, always different yet always graceful, my face serious, my body bending and twisting, hoops spinning on my waist and legs and arms, like a Chinese acrobat with hula hoops.

I tart it up for Parts Unknown. Hair glitter and makeup that makes me look like a pale cat and when I come out, slow and somber, I'm in a slinky prom dress. I limber up, usually with five hoops spinning, aloof-cat me hardly moving as I trance out, then the spotlight dims and when it brightens again, I'm in one of my many sparkly catsuits.

Strange? Yep. But girls and boys, women and men, like my kind of strange. Parts Unknown, which also has a Mongolian strong man, an ancient trapeze lady, and a Mexican family who ride motorcycles inside of a steel globe, travels with a carnival and we do county and state fairs all over the southeast. Most of the time I'm the girl on the billboards and when word gets around that I'm not around, like when my mom died, the seats are half full. Yes, I'm so almost famous Cirque offered me a job for a lot more money. I passed. Loyalty to the weirdo family of Part Unknown is part of it. But of most importance is Wayne. I'm quitting and marrying Wayne as soon as Clarissa is ready.

Clarissa? Where do I begin? She's pretty and fit, sweet and adventurous, a nineteen-year-old me I've been told. She's so much like me, wants to be me, one recent day she showed up in the Parts Unknown Airstream we share with her strawberry hair stacked on her head and mischief on her face. She laughed. Made me ask what was so funny. Then, as I fussed with some black-eyed Susans I was putting into a vase, she pirouetted like a ballerina and showed me her freshly inked red lotus flower.

And while she'll probably be one of those lucky women who hold onto their starry-eyed optimism forever, Clarissa's going through some big and perplexing changes, trying hard to stay true to her hardscrabble roots while also having to admit, as I had to admit, that, yeah, the wider world outside of the hollers and nowhere towns might be Sodom and Gomorrah, but Sodom and Gomorrah, each and every day, feels more and more like home sweet home.

I'm a country girl. Clarissa's a backcountry girl from West Virginia. A glass of Merlot loosens her tongue, gets her talking about a life alien to me, such as making moonshine and yearning for a steaming bowl of possum stew. That's backcountry holler living. As for her Parts Unknown act, she can do almost everything I can do with hula hoops. She just doesn't have my God-given flexibility and, at least at first, she had trouble owning the audience when she was in the spotlight.

I was thinking about Clarissa at Shenandoah National Park. We'd finished the Virginia circuit and I refused to go home, still rattled about what I had done to Rebecca. I've never attacked anyone and, yeah, karma saw that. Many others did, too, as various videos were all over Facebook, which I was not on. What had come over me? It had almost been like a blackout that drunks talk about. Was it going to happen again? Was I losing my mind?

Wanting to get my mind off my troubled mind, I returned to Clarissa. I was at Skyland, sitting on the patio, happy to be somewhere without reception, my phone in the glove compartment of my rental car, staring down the Blue Ridge Mountains, drinking chai tea, and sharing my bagel with a chipmunk. Clarissa and I, after agreeing she'd never be me, had been tinkering with her act. "Be yourself," I advised her. And that's what happened. My act was sensual. Hers became almost erotic. I was an aloof dominatrix. She became a bubbly stripper. Dancing and hooping to the Great American Songbook—I especially liked when she hooped to "Summer Wind"—she was all smiles and bittersweet froth. Her most popular segment, at least for the men, was when she'd sit on a man's lap and hoop from there. She called that "her hula hoop lap dance."

Pretty soon, we both hoped, she'd be the face and body on the billboards. I tossed another bagel chunk to the chipmunk, switched my thoughts to Wayne. He was supposed to join me and we were going to backpack the Appalachian Trail for three days. Mother Nature tends to clear my head. A broken leg on another sheriff changed those plans. So it was just me and day hikes. All good. Just not as good as Wayne and spring water and sleeping with the bears and owls would have been.

I sipped my chai. Watched a goldfinch glide over a spray of woodland sunflowers and lost in my thoughts about Wayne and Clarissa, I was almost happy. I was so deep inside my head that I was unaware someone was behind me until he cleared his throat. The next thing I knew I was squeezing the life out of Wayne.

"Wow, wonderful. How'd you get off? Who cares, right? We can still do an overnighter on the AT. Bearfence works for me."

Something was wrong. He was as stiff as a wooden bear and not hugging me back. I slowly unwrapped and stepped back, and as my heart ramped up, I looked up at his worried face. He didn't make me wait. Said it right away.

"Someone shot Rebecca in the face."

* * * *

I'm flawed and I have my weaknesses but I'm a good woman. Not only do I do my outreach program, I do all I can for Parts Unknown. I smile and sell snow cones before the show and after my performance I sign autographs and pose for pictures. More than anyone, Wayne knows I'm righteous, knows the public Allison is the same as the private Allison. So to see the doubt in his eyes as I stumbled away from him and knocked over my tea, really hurt. I'm not saying he was certain I shot Rebecca. But he sure wasn't sure I didn't.

After my head cleared, I asked Wayne to take me to the Kentucky State Police. He called ahead and set up my interrogation. The detectives waiting for me at the Lexington station were two fortyish women. They smiled at me like two plump cats eager to dine on a mouse as they escorted me into the bland interrogation room. I sat down behind a chipped Formica table in a plastic chair. They were on the other side in ratty swivel chairs. The tiny room reeked of sorrow. They turned on the camera and read me my Miranda rights. I refused a lawyer. They got right to it. No chit-chat.

"Did you threaten to rip off Rebecca Sweeney's face?"

"Yes."

"Did you shoot Rebecca Sweeney in the face?"

"No."

"Do you know who did?"

"No."

"Where were you on October eighteenth?"

"Shenandoah National Park, hiking the AT. I hiked from Lewis Mountain to Big Meadows that day. I also bought breakfast and dinner at the Pollock dining room at Skyland each day. I used my debit card."

The two detectives looked at each other and smiled. Road trip. Then after having a tech run my debit card and finding the bare bones of my story checked out, they told me I could go but be back in three days.

Wayne and I drove back to Middlesboro and I slipped back into my little black funeral dress and held my head high as I stood beside my father, who initially had looked at me like he was next on his crazy daughter's hit list. It was a quiet burial, as the police kept the media and the trolls away from the grave. Outside the cemetery gate, however, the media shouted questions and the trolls barked and brayed and called me a killer. All they got was my emotionless face behind tinted glass.

I behaved at the funeral breakfast.

* * * *

Rebecca was on my father's porch, looking great in her Lululemon ensemble, doing yoga, when a .22 bullet, shot from the wooded area below the house, hit her between the eyes. And, yes, she also looked great in her coffin. Much like she did when she was alive, except for less makeup and some spackling where the bullet entered.

I went back to the state police and not only did I pass my polygraph, the ballistic testing on the deadly bullet proved it hadn't come from any of our family guns. My debit card and signature also backed up my story, and the waitress who brought me my morning oatmeal nodded at my picture and said I was "very pretty and very pleasant." I had about eight hours of unaccounted time each day at Shenandoah when I was on the trails. But to drive to Middlesboro, whack Rebecca, then get back to use my debit card for dinner at Skyland only worked if I was shot out of a cannon, both ways.

Eyewitness News led the media charge, roasting the befuddled state police, bemoaning each night the loss of their beloved Rebecca. And while those two plump cats were still certain I had pulled the trigger, they had reached a temporary dead end. So they moved onto Wayne and then onto my dad. Both had been working at the time of the murder. Both, however, also had unaccounted time around the time of the shooting. Both, nevertheless, passed the polygraph. Then they began working their way down the guest list at the funeral breakfast and the troll list on Facebook. They were taken off the case before they got too far. Two men, Kentucky's so-called best, took over and brought me back in.

I was touring Louisiana at the time and we had to put on more shows. A murder mystery, especially when the star of the show is guilty in the minds of many, is good for business. Kentucky's best had retested the bullet and while the results were the same—it had come from an unknown gun—they grilled me about buying a black-market rifle. I hadn't and told them so. Then we went down the rabbit hole of blackouts and body doubles. But most of my interrogations were the same questions. They just kept me in that sad and bland room much longer; six hours one day, and had me repeat my story over and over, in minute detail, right down to the chipmunk who shared my bagel. They found no contradictions. All I did was continue to tell the truth: I did not kill Rebecca and I did not know who had.

Kentucky's best then worked over Wayne and my dad about their unaccounted time. There, however, wasn't anything suspicious about it. It was just time at work alone, time when another set of eyeballs weren't on them. Nothing came of it.

Eventually, some decided that Rebecca's death was just a strange coincidence, like Wayne and I seeing that karma bumper sticker. Those who believe in almost impossible odds believe a good ol' boy plinking racoons out of trees accidently put a bullet through Rebecca's forehead.

"Stranger things have happened," the coincidence believers say.

I even half believed it for a while.

But that's not what happened.

* * * *

"Life goes on," Wayne assured me.

And it did.

The Kentucky Troopers and Eyewitness News, the trolls and the gossipers, eventually lost interest in me. Wayne, as expected, aced the state police exam and became a trooper six months after Rebecca was put into the dirt. Dad's love life was also in the dirt. Not sure if he lost interest after the wham-bam deaths of my mother and his Barbie doll or if women refused to hook up with a man with such bad karma. Wayne, who looked like an extra-large movie star in his gray trooper shirt and black Stetson, was assigned to Louisville and we found this cute upper apartment with a turret room. We also eloped. Maybe someday we'd have a reception in Middlesboro. Fifty years sounds about right to me.

Also that spring, with Mother Nature and my new life in full bloom, I passed the baton—or the hoop—to Clarissa. Her act would never be as hypnotic as mine. Yet it was more fun. Most likely, no one would even remember my name in a month. Fine with me. Life goes on. I kept it together for my final performance, which was near Shenandoah National Park, then fell to pieces with Clarissa in our fragrant and candlelit Airstream. The lilacs bouquets Clarissa collected and the shots of moonshine we knocked back glued some of me back together and we hugged each other fiercely.

"Karma saw it, karma liked it," I whispered in her ear.

I lingered my moist lips on her ear and then eventually stepped back—just a bit—and Clarissa tenderly brushed her fingertips across my cheek.

"It was like shooting an ornery possum, was all," starry-eyed Clarissa said to my quivering cat face.

Then we shared our sly and secret smile.

✗

R.S. Morgan is an award-winning writer who has been publishing fiction and non-fiction nationally since 1983. His fiction first appeared in *Mike Shayne Mystery Magazine*. Most recently, in 2020, *Mystery Tribune* published his crime fiction and in 2017, *Mystery Weekly Magazine* published his literary suspense as its featured cover story. He is also a retired UAW skilled tradesman and a retired first responder.

DEATH WILL GIVE
YOU A REASON

ELIZABETH ZELVIN

Gotta cancel dinner, Cindy texted Bruce. *Caught a case.*

Murder in the Park?

Cindy's detective squad worked out of the Central Park Precinct. It wasn't always as interesting as murder.

Body floating in Harlem Meer.

Cool. For you, not the body. Later. Love you.

Good man, she thought. He knew what mattered: not the best Moroccan food in Manhattan or the fact that they hadn't seen each other in three days. The longer Bruce stayed sober, the more empathy he developed. He'd become—the Yiddish word was a *mensch*. No, it wasn't cool to be a floater, dank and bloated, trailing the kind of clothes that churches gave to the homeless because they couldn't sell them at a rummage sale, not even at a rock bottom price.

"Cinders! Get over here!" Her partner Natali's voice drove Bruce from her mind.

The scene, at the northeast corner of the Park, had been secured before she got there. The CSU techs were already at work. The doc from the Medical Examiner's office was squinting at her thermometer.

"The witnesses know nothing," Natali said. "Coupla dog walkers. The dogs all started barking when the body bumped up against the bank."

"Photos?" Cindy asked. Some bystander always had an iPhone.

"*Professional* dog walkers," Natali snarled. "Six leashes in each hand. Labs, beagles, terriers, dachshunds. *Two dozen* witnesses. If we had someone who spoke Bark, we might have eyewitnesses instead of shit. By the time anyone else realized the circus had come to town, the leashes were all tangled up in each other and doggy legs and corpse's arms."

"What did you do, arrest the dogs?"

"I was tempted," Natali said. "The idiots tried to pull him out—without letting go of the leashes. They seemed to think I'd give them a medal for obeying the leash law. By the time the uniforms arrived, the scene was already compromised."

"Let's see the deceased," Cindy said.

"Go ahead. I already looked. I sniffed him up and down too. The pooches inspired me."

"Anything of interest?"

"Alcohol and weed."

"Lake or marijuana?"

"Both. White guy, very white. Looked like he'd bled out."

"Where was the wound?"

"I didn't spot it. Under the clothes, maybe. Let's let the ME get on with it. We'll learn a lot more at the morgue in the morning."

* * * *

Dead people never looked quite like the living. Those who had been murdered, less than most. The way they lay, limbs scattered. Murder caught them utterly off guard. After the autopsy, with their innards weighed and described in the pathologist's precise, dry tones—it was a knack, like giving evidence in court—however neatly their outsides got stitched up again, you could hardly call them people anymore. Although the room was brightly lit, the body was bluish white, as if it still floated in Harlem Meer. Cindy stared at it until Natali snapped his fingers under her nose.

"Cinders! Wake up!"

"Sorry," she said.

"You were in a trance," he said. "No ID on the vic, but he didn't drown. It was a knife wound."

"So he bled out."

"Yeah, the cut started under the arm, and the blood got washed away in the Meer. C'mon, let's get back to the barn. Download everything from there."

Natali drove. Cindy stared out through midtown traffic at the crowd, all those people chock full of the warmth and sweetness and fire that drained out of the dead.

"Whaddaya daydreaming about?" he asked. "I know you got that big AA thing coming up."

"My anniversary. I have to tell my story. What it was like, what happened, and what it's like now, ten years clean and sober. It's a big deal. A lot of people who watched me crawl out of the muck will be there. People who are proud of me. People I don't lie to."

"I'm impressed," Natali said. "Jesus, Mary, and Joseph, I don't think any of the people who are proud of me are people I don't lie to. Everyone commits sins of omission, don't they?"

"Don't worry about it," she said. "I'm thinking about the case, OK?"

"I know you are."

Natali spun the wheel of the unmarked car left, then right and in a wide arc north along the Park Road East, where the foliage was beginning to show its colors in spite of the unseasonable warmth. Yellow, scarlet, purple, russet, a wooded oasis in the heart of the city with the NYPD, their precinct, at the heart of the heart, keeping its citizens alive. Unless they came too late.

"I'll make sure you get the hours off for your meeting," he said, "whatever you need. Just tell me when. Everyone knows you give the job all you've got."

"Thanks, Natali," Cindy said. "That means a lot to me."

It didn't matter why you drank. Once you started, you left *why* far behind. You thought drinking made you happy, but you were running from memories and regrets. You'd do anything to douse the pain. Spacing out at the morgue, Cindy had thought she was thinking about the past, the way you did on milestone anniversaries. Most women in recovery had catastrophic histories with men. Some, not Cindy, had been molested, raped, battered. The rest, including Cindy, had just had bad relationships, given away their power to every worthless man they loved. Did they leave? Oh, no. Why not? Because they *loooooved* him. In sobriety, they realized booze and drugs had been involved in every single decision they'd made in those relationships.

Stupid young Cindy had believed that giving away her power, *wanting* to be subsumed, consumed, burn bright, and crumble into ash and dust proved that it was really love. Wasn't love the biggest high of all? And Shane, her first, had been that smitten Cindy's biggest love.

Shane's parents and hers rented adjacent summer beach cottages on Long Island. It was love at first sight at age five. She laughed at his long curly hair and called him a lion cub. He hit her with his blue plastic shovel. At eight he threw sand in her eye. She punched him and knocked out a tooth. It had been wiggling anyway. They built sandcastles and combed the beach for shells. At twelve, they skateboarded and body surfed and raced each other so far out to sea that once the lifeguards spotted a shark and not only blew their whistles but came in after them, furious.

At fifteen, they got stoned and made love in the dunes. Pot brought out a fey quality in Shane. He wanted to join the Army, which he didn't think would interfere with his being a pothead. Too bad he turned out to be right about that. The Army claimed it made men. In Shane's case, it made a larger, stronger, more willful though still beguiling boy who only wanted to get high with her and make love. That part was all right. But Shane was medicating his PTSD with heroin, and she could see a bad time coming.

They had a lot of fights.

"Why don't you grow up!" she screamed at him once, beside herself with rage.

"Why should I?" he'd said. "Give me one good reason."

He walked out of the room before she could think of a retort.

She couldn't have given him an answer then, and he'd walked out of her life for good not too long afterward. She needed to grow up herself before she could articulate the reasons. And she needed to get clean and sober before she could grow up. Getting drunk and listening to sad songs didn't help the first time or the thousandth.

She'd thought she was thinking about all that this morning, staring at the body with its neat Y stitching down the torso. But when Natali snapped his fingers, she'd realized she was looking down at Shane.

"Sarge," she said now.

Natali put his arms behind his head and tilted his chair onto its back legs, a bad habit he refused to believe could ever hurt him.

"Yes, more coffee, please," he said. "We've been working half an hour, and my mug is empty. But wait! You only call me that in front of the team. I deduce it's serious. What's up?"

"I can ID the victim," she said.

"Huh? We had a conversation not an hour ago about sins of omission."

"The guy is someone I knew when we were kids," Cindy said, "and hadn't seen in twenty years. He'd changed so much I had no idea till right before we left the morgue."

"But when you did, you didn't say, 'Natali, whoa, I know this guy, let's order some forensics so we won't lose any time.'"

"I was rattled! I needed an hour to get my head together, that's all. I'm telling you now. His name is Shane Dougherty. I'll run him through the system myself if you still trust me."

"Whaddaya trying to get out of the scut work? You get the forensics and you run him."

"Right away."

"You said kids. You knew this Dougherty guy since you were how much?"

"We met when we were five."

"Ohhh." Natali rested one elbow on his desk and tapped the side of his head with a ballpoint pen. "Very young love. Now I'm having trouble believing you recognized the guy at all."

"We grew up together," Cindy said. "Well, I grew up. He didn't."

"A regular Peter Pan, huh? Are you telling me you didn't sleep with him?"

"I didn't say that."

"We won't put it in the report, damn it. You think up a story, I'll back you. But you tell me the whole truth and nothing but the truth."

"Natali, that is so above and beyond I don't know how to thank you."

"Pastrami sandwiches from the good place from now till Christmas," he said, "and we never mention it again."

"We were each other's first, and it mattered a lot. We fought, he left, and that was it for twenty years. I never expected to see him again. But it's Shane. Ask me anything you want to know."

"I will," he said.

* * * *

"It's a dead end, Sarge," Cindy said at the morning team meeting two days later. "Dougherty's in the system, but the trail ends eight, nine years ago."

"What did you get before that?"

"Early on, auto theft," she said, "bumped down to joyriding. Disorderly conduct, resisting arrest, no felonies. DWIs."

"Drugs?" one of the other detectives asked. "Possession? Dealing?"

"No convictions," she said. "The parents bought him lawyers, but they cut him off a year before he left the city, if that's what he did."

"He could have been incarcerated," someone said.

"Not in New York State," Cindy said. "Maybe in another jurisdiction."

"Any reason you haven't talked with the parents yet?" Natali asked.

"The only good one," Cindy said. "They're dead."

"What else, Cinders?" Natali said.

"He was in the Army. The VA must have records, but it was more than twenty years ago."

"Not top priority," Natali said. "Hold it in reserve."

"He had some treatment on and off," Cindy said, "alcohol and substance abuse, but he never finished any program he started. A few detoxes and low-end rehabs and a halfway house. I'll check those out. No pillhead movie stars, Solczak, so don't bother volunteering."

A halfway house, for recovering people moving from residential treatment to the real world, was a cage with a wide open door. Shane might have been less guarded there than in a more structured institution. She might learn something, if anyone who'd known him was still there.

* * * *

Cindy drove to Canarsie, but Shane would have had to take the obscure L train to the end of the line. People thought of Canarsie as the armpit of Brooklyn, but it was a seaside neighborhood on the shore of Jamaica Bay that had seen both better days and worse. In the Roaring Twenties, during Prohibition, it had been splashy Boardwalk Empire, where the gangsters raised a thousand glasses with the cops.

The halfway house was still there. The house manager was a woman in her fifties whose kind brown eyes lit up when Cindy said Shane's name. She had fading brown hair streaked with gray pulled back in a loose braid and a comfortable body you could imagine a child sinking into like a beanbag chair. She wore gray sweatpants, flip-flops, and a beautiful loose tunic in a Guatemalan weave.

"I won't take too much of your time, Ms. Estrada," Cindy said.

"Please, call me Luna. And sit down. I'll make you some tea. It's no trouble. The men won't come in for another hour."

"Thanks. I hoped I would find someone who remembered Shane Dougherty, but I'm still surprised. You can confirm this is when he stayed here?" She read off the date from her notes.

"That was the only time he was a resident," Ms. Estrada said. "But he came back."

"To visit you?"

"It was against the rules, but I don't regret it. He was sweet and such a pretty boy. I wasn't young. At that age, you want to believe it when someone says you're beautiful. I didn't, but I wanted to. At least I had a figure. Now, forget it. Here's your tea. Have some of our rooftop honey, it's from Brooklyn bees."

"When did you last see Shane?"

The halfway house kitchen was a peaceful oasis. A beam of dusty late-afternoon light slanted through the window, evading the approaching night.

"Is he back? I would love to see him! Not as a lover—I'm an old woman now. But that's not what matters, is it?"

"What matters, then?" Cindy asked.

"We got sober together," Luna said. "That is a bond that never breaks. Those moments of honesty, even if they don't last long, are as intimate as sex. You must think I'm talking nonsense."

Hi, Luna, my name is Cindy, and I'm an alcoholic. You're talking perfect sense. She wanted to hug this lovely woman and weep with her for Shane. But she didn't do that on the job.

"How did you meet?"

"In a program. I stayed, he left. I got him to come with me to AA meetings whenever I could. Then we both got in here."

"It wasn't always all men?" Cindy asked.

"Not until the following year," Luna said. "I thought I'd have to leave."

"Oh?"

"Shane and I never got caught, but other residents who fraternized did. Their solution was to send the women away."

"Except you?"

"They offered me assistant manager. I had two years recovery. I was ready for a job. The cook was a Guatemalan from my village. So I stayed when the women residents left."

"It doesn't seem fair," Cindy said. "Did you stay in touch with any of them? Were they angry?"

"They were at first," Luna said, "but the facility where they transferred was brand new. The ones I still ran into at AA meetings got to like it, and so did I."

"That sounds like a happy ending for you," Cindy said.

It was time to break the news. It was her job, but she found herself stalling.

"Those are beautiful colors on your tunic," she said.

"Made in my village." Luna ran a caressing hand down her tunic.

"One of a kind, I bet," Cindy said. "Can you tell me when you last saw Shane?"

"Years ago," Luna said, "right before he went to California."

Shane had always talked about California. Skateboarding on Venice Beach. The Pacific, where the sun set over the water. The ocean that was blue instead of dull Atlantic green. She'd said, not always nicely, that maybe one day he'd stop talking about it and go. But she hadn't believed he would.

"If he is back, please tell me!" Luna said. "Is he in trouble? I'd like to help if I can."

"Ms. Estrada." Cindy took her hands, not the textbook way for a cop to break the news. "Luna, I'm so sorry. Shane Dougherty is dead. I'm investigating his murder."

The residents started arriving while Luna was still crying. They took over the tasks of comforting her and making fresh tea. Luna took Cindy's card and promised to look up the dates of all Shane's visits and email her the information "as soon as I pull myself together."

"Can you think of anything else that might help? Why he might have come back? Where he might have gone? Anyone he ever mentioned? Someone he loved or hated? Someone he might have wanted to see?"

And wouldn't it be a custard pie in the face if Luna said, *Oh, yes, Shane said there was a girl called Cindy. Shane said that when he left, he forgot to say, Fuck you.* That wouldn't happen. Besides, that girl had nothing to do with Detective Wendy Cenedella of the Central Park Precinct, NYPD, phone and email on her card.

"There's nothing," Luna said. "No, wait. He had a sister. His little sister. He felt guilty because she got heavy into drugs after he turned her on. He'd go to visit her and then get drunk and sob. I'll think of her name in a minute."

The name came back to Cindy a second before Luna recalled it. How could she have forgotten? A fairylike child, five years younger, barely born when she and Shane first met, drifting after them laughing, calling, "Wait up, Shane!"

"Something starry or shushy. Shelly? Aster? Shari? Shasta! That was it, Shasta. You'll find her, won't you? If she made it into recovery, could you let me know? We could grieve for Shane together."

"I can't promise anything," Cindy said. "But if there's a way, we'll see."

As she opened the door, already gone, Luna's sad voice followed her out.

"I always hoped he would come back."

* * * *

"We're finally getting somewhere," Cindy said. "Once I find Shasta Dougherty, there'll be other leads. Estrada thought he visited the sister up until he left New York. Maybe they stayed in touch. She might have known he was coming back. What if he was staying with her? What if she can tell us all about his plans?"

"What if, what if?" Natali said. "Legwork, Detective, legwork. Find me a person of interest."

Shasta had more arrests on her record than Shane, because a girl who needed drugs had one surefire commodity. In Cindy's experience, which ranged from arresting prostitutes in appalling circumstances to hearing the candid reminiscences of women who'd gotten out and had decades clean and sober, there were no happy hookers. Hooking was an insult to body and soul. Cindy scrolled through the law's impression of Shasta at sixteen, seventeen, nineteen, twenty-two, each time more skeletal, with long untended hair and bruised skin. Violence, malnutrition, hopelessness had all had a hand in stripping the freshness from her face. Mug shots didn't show the track marks that must have clustered along her veins more thickly every year.

Yet Shasta hadn't given up. She'd been in and out of treatment programs several times, and she'd stuck with them better than Shane. The first had been a program for incarcerated women at Rikers. Then outpatient programs around the city—the Bronx, Brooklyn, Inwood, the Lower East Side. Cindy visited them all. Non-profits funded by the State, they took client confidentiality seriously. They could neither confirm nor deny, as they put it, that they'd ever had a Shasta Dougherty on their rolls. But Cindy was adept at catching a flickering eye or a tightening lip—a client who'd been Shasta's friend, an inexperienced counselor, an office aide with a soft spot for an appealing waif. She'd ask as many questions as she could before someone broke it up.

There was a break of several years when Shasta's name didn't show up. Maybe she was going to AA and doing well. Or had she left the city along with Shane? Then there she was again, only three months ago—drunk and disorderly and resisting arrest, which was a Class A misdemeanor and could mean a year in jail, especially with her priors. Shasta had shown up with a lawyer and been referred instead to an outpatient program in East Harlem. Was that when Shane came back to town? Had his reappearance in her life triggered her relapse? Maybe Shasta was still attending that program. If she was ninety days clean and sober, long enough to recover mental clarity—or as Bruce would put it, get her brains back—she'd have answers.

This time, it was a grizzled Puerto Rican with a gold tooth at the front desk who said, "You might want to talk to the skinny sister with the tats."

"Thanks, I appreciate it."

"Aretha, you got a minute?"

The girl strolled toward her, fiddling with her beaded bracelets and talking into her phone. Neither Cindy nor the desk man betrayed by a blink that they knew each other as "Hi, I'm Cindy, I'm an alcoholic" and "I'm Ernesto, grateful recovering alcoholic and drug addict." The meeting where she saw him two or three times a month was close to the Park but not too close to the station. So far, she'd never run into any cops who knew her.

"Whassup, Ernesto?"

"You hear from your friend Shasta today, Aretha?" Ernesto said.

"Not since she ran outta here the other day," Aretha said. "Why you wanna know?"

"I don't like to see someone doin' so well throw it all away," he said. "You talk to her, tell her maybe it's not too late."

"That all you got to say?" Aretha asked.

Ernesto ducked his head toward Cindy.

"This lady wants to talk to you. Now, you be nice to her. If you don't, you don't get to taste my Rosita's *pasteles* at Christmas."

"It's a long way till Christmas," Aretha said. "What makes you think I'm still gonna be here?"

"Rosita's *pasteles* are worth it." Ernesto's gold tooth gleamed. "You only gotta stay clean and be nice to this lady."

"Thanks, Ernesto," Cindy said, herding Aretha toward the door of the clinic.

They emerged into bright sunshine and made their way down the street to a *bodega* whose awning cast a little shade. Aretha lit a cigarette.

"So who'm I being nice to, lady?"

"Cenedella," Cindy said, leaning back against the brick wall of the *bodega*. "I'm with Central Park NYPD." *Practically not a cop.* "Your friend Shasta isn't in any trouble." *So don't worry that* you're *in trouble.* "But I have bad news for her. Do you have a contact number?"

"What bad news?" Aretha asked. "Is Daisy OK?"

"Who's Daisy, Aretha?"

"If you don't know, never mind," Aretha said. "Like, you wanna text her? I tried that. She don't answer."

"Are you and Shasta close friends?" Cindy asked.

"Yeah, we been friends for years."

"I'd like to help," Cindy said, "but first I need to get hold of her."

"Oh, yeah?" Aretha said. "What can you do? A Park cop."

"Well, I am a detective," Cindy said.

"No shit. Why you need her so bad?"

"I'll tell you, so you can understand how important it is. I need to tell her that her brother is dead."

"Her brother!" Aretha's eyebrows shot up. "No shit!"

"Did you know Shasta had a brother?"

"No! I thought I knew everything about her, but she never mentioned him. Wait, izzat who that scuzzy guy was? He wanted to see her, but he was wasted so they wouldn't let him in."

"What scuzzy guy? A man came to the clinic to see Shasta? When was that?"

"Three days ago."

The day they'd found Shane's body.

"They wouldn't even say if she was there," she said. "You saw how they are. But he kept yelling, 'Shasta! Shasta!' till she came running out. She like kept hitting out till she made it out the door. Elbows, knees, teeth—well, she woulda. Couldn't nobody have stopped her. She mighta went off with him, but maybe not."

"Why not?" Cindy asked.

"That boy was more than drunk. He was strung out. He mighta just wanted money and took off when she gave it to him." A glorious voice broke in, saying someone made her feel like a natural woman. "Gotta get this. Shasta! Where are you, Shas? I've been so worried! Listen—"

It took all Cindy's self-discipline not to seize Aretha by both wrists and grab control of the phone.

"Just tell her that you're there for her," she whispered. "She'll get too upset if you break the news on the phone. Ask where she is and can you meet her. You don't have to tell her about me yet, sounds like she's freaked out already."

"Calm down, girl! You gotta calm down!" Aretha said.

Cindy read her taut throat and frantic hands as trying to convey by sheer willpower, *If you shriek like that, this lady detective is gonna hear every word you say.*

"Thass better," Aretha said. "I *know*, Shas, but you gotta deal with it. Of *course* it sucks. Would I say it didn't suck? What kinda friend you think I am?"

Cindy said the Serenity Prayer and texted Natali an update.

Good work, he texted back. *Need backup?*

For a witness I used to babysit?

She and Shane hadn't been attentive sitters, too absorbed in themselves and each other. The Doughertys hadn't been attentive parents, either. She still couldn't think why she hadn't remembered Shasta. She'd always tagged along. *Wait up, Shane!*

"Like you don't know how that ends," Aretha said.

What were they talking about?

"You score and you're outta the program, and whatcha gonna do next? Don't start cryin' again, it don't make nothin' better."

Oh, God. Was that a hypothetical, or was Shasta back on drugs? If she was, was Shane responsible? Had he tried to stop her? Had he tried to help her? Had his descent on the clinic triggered her relapse? It was time to intervene, whether Aretha liked it or not.

She reached out for the phone. Aretha held it above her head and glared at her.

"Aretha, work with me," Cindy said. "She doesn't know her brother's dead. That's not fair. Get her to say she'll meet you. And don't spook her!" *Don't say "cop."*

"I am!" Aretha said. "Gimme a minute! Whatcha say, Shas? Daisy's what? Daisy's Hello Kitty bag?"

Hello *Kitty*? And who the hell was Daisy?

"They won't let you back in, you know that. If I go in, they'll make me go to group. I'm *not* mad at you. Yeah, I'm gonna help you. Yeah, I love you unconditionally even when you shitfaced. I *do* believe you got it in you to get clean again. Look, I got an idea, but I gotta work it out. I'll get your fuckin' Hello Kitty and see you in an hour. Where you wanna meet?"

The Park, Cindy tapped into her phone. *Brick house on lake, Fifth Ave & 110th.*

She couldn't send it without knowing Aretha's number, but she held up her screen. Aretha nodded. Cindy brought up a photo of the building she meant, the Charles A. Dana Discovery Center on Harlem Meer. To her relief, Aretha fell in with the plan.

"Nemmind, I got a place. I'll text you a picture. I'll bring the bag. Shas, I *got* this."

"Now it's time to earn whatever help you want from me," Cindy said. "I have a job to do."

"OK, but you gotta call Ernesto first. He's gotta tell my counselor I'm assisting in police business, *not* trouble, and you'll gimme evidence—if you *are* a real cop—like, write a note. And you can buy me a double iced caramel macchiato and a Boston Kreme donut and a strawberry frosted at that Dunkin across the street before I'll say a word. We got an hour, and I eat fast."

Five minutes later, Aretha chugged the last of her macchiato and crunched an ice cube.

"No more stalling, Tattoo Girl," Cindy said. "Who's Daisy?"

"Daisy's Shasta's daughter. Shas must of looked just like her when she was eight. Shas don't want Daisy to suffer for her mistakes or make a single one a them herself. She's outta her mind right now. Daisy'll give it to her good for what she calls messin' up—Shas makes her speak like a lady. That kid's so cute and smart. She's like a little grownup. She can shop and clean and cook, and you should see her act like she's the mom and Shasta's the kid."

"But she likes Hello Kitty."

"Well, yeah, she's still a little girl. Shas left Daisy's Hello Kitty bag in there, and if she don't bring it home, that'll be one more thing Daisy'll be mad at her about. But if I go in, they ain't gonna let me take it and run. You have to go."

"I can't," Cindy said.

They wouldn't even admit Shasta had been there unless she came back with a warrant, and she was not going anywhere. She couldn't let this chance slip away.

"I'll give you my card and write a note, and you'll go in. I'll wait here for you."

"Maybe I can get Ernesto to slip me past the desk," Aretha said. "That'll be quicker."

"What else did Shasta tell you?"

"How do smart girls get so dumb? Junkies and hookers aren't always stupid, lady detective. Did you know that? But when they give their power to a man? Good as dumb pills. Doesn't matter who the man is. Pimp, dealer, boyfriend who swears he's gonna get you out of the life. Now brother. She didn't know he was back in the city. She *says* she went after him to try to talk him into getting into treatment. Like being Mother Theresa was her top priority."

"Not to stop him making a scene?"

"That too. But duh, what happened is he had coke on him and they did a line together and so long recovery."

"We need to get going," Cindy said. "One more quick question. Did Shasta ever say who Daisy's father was?"

"How could she? We were both heavy into smack at the time and turning tricks. She got knocked up right after she went out again. Do you know how many johns get off on fucking a pregnant woman? It sucked, that whole year. I was glad I had a friend, so you be nice to Shasta when we get there. Here, gimme your card and write that note. Huh, you are a real cop. NYPD and all. Detective Ce-ne-dell-a."

"They do have violent crime in Central Park," Cindy said. "Now scoot."

"Here, hold my phone," Aretha said. "Then they can't confiscate it to make me stay. Wait, here's a selfie of me with her and Daisy. We both stayed clean six months that time. Daisy was five. Don't she look just like Shasta?"

Cindy felt sick. The little girl looked even more like Shane. When Shasta was five, she'd had pale gold curls like an angel—not tawny curls like a lion cub, like Daisy and Shane.

Twenty minutes later, Aretha came out waving the small faux-plastic Hello Kitty handbag with its perky red bow. She parted with it reluctantly.

"You can't come with me," Cindy said. "I don't have time to argue. Thanks to your selfie, I know what Shasta looks like. So get back into that clinic. Don't blow your own shot at staying clean."

Natali would say she needed backup. He'd be right, but she couldn't wait. She started toward the Park at a steady jog, planning what to say. She didn't want Shasta to bolt. She wouldn't lead with her gold shield. Start with Aretha's name and the Hello Kitty bag, then the childhood connection. Didn't Shasta remember her babysitter from the beach, Shane's friend? Hadn't Shane *ever* mentioned her?

But it was Detective Cenedella who got Shasta seated on a bench near the Discovery Center with her fingers wrapped around a cup of coffee and settled next to her.

"I'm so sorry about Shane," she said. "I was very fond of him at one time. But things changed. He changed."

"Did he?" Shasta stared out across the Meer.

"It doesn't matter now," Cindy said. "I do need to ask you a few questions. When he came to the clinic, how did that happen?"

"I don't know," Shasta said. "I didn't even know he was in New York."

"What was the last address you had for him?"

"None. I mean, when he left the city, he said he was going to California, and he never contacted me. I figured that was it. When I was using, I couldn't think about it. And when I was clean, I had Daisy to think about. My daughter."

"The Hello Kitty girl." Cindy smiled. "Your friend Aretha showed me her picture. She's lovely."

"She's smart, too," Shasta said. "She's going to *be* somebody. I just have to get back on track so I can be there for her. I can't afford to let any of Shane's messes get in my way."

"What kind of messes did Shane make?"

"That day, when they wouldn't let him in the door, I didn't want him making a scene and getting me in trouble. That's why I went out after him, to shut him up. By the time I caught up with him, he was halfway to the Park, so that's where we went."

Wait up, Shane!

"He said he wanted to talk. I figured the sooner I let him spit out whatever he'd come to say, the sooner he'd go away. I took him here because I knew it would be quiet and we could get coffee."

"You weren't glad to see your brother?" Cindy asked.

"He was *wasted*!" Shasta said. "I didn't want anything to do with him! I had my ninety-day coin. I was *clean*. He said he wanted us to be a family again, but it didn't take long before he was asking how much money I could spare. I shouldn't have mentioned Daisy to him. But I don't keep her a secret. Why should I? She's the light of my life. He asked me a million questions about her. He would have been all over her. As if I would have let him near her!"

"And when did you get high with him?"

"I didn't! What makes you think I did?"

"Didn't you tell Aretha that you'd scored? And that was why you couldn't come back to the treatment program?"

"Ohh, on the *phone*," Shasta said. "I only told her that to get her off my case. Shane was drunk already. He did some lines of coke he had on him. He wanted me to, but I said no. I told him to go in the men's room. I didn't want to get caught on possession and fuck up my life all over again. So he did, and while he was in there, I left."

"Where did you go?"

"I wandered around the Park, no place special."

"If you were still clean," Cindy asked, "why didn't you go back to the clinic?"

"I was going to," Shasta said. "I just needed some time to think first. I needed to get my slimy brother off my skin."

"What do you mean?"

"Like when you meditate," Shasta said. "Maybe you don't meditate. I set an intention. I would not let my scumbag brother destroy my life again!"

"What did he do to you, Shasta?" Cindy asked. "How did he destroy your life?"

"People used to say, 'Your brother is so weird,'" Shasta said. "Once you've met enough alcoholics and drug addicts, you realize in some ways they're all the same. *We're* the same. Predictable, as long as we keep using. Recovery's the only way to break the pattern. Recovery can save us. It can make us surprising."

"What did he do to you, Shasta?"

"Nine years ago," she said, "I had my own place. I'd been clean about a year and a half. I had a job I liked. I was *fine*. Shane shows up drunk and tells me he's leaving for California. He has a bottle of Grey Goose. When I won't drink with him, he says, more for him, then. He has a couple and starts asking me for money, just like every single time. Halfway down, he starts reminiscing about our childhood. Only he remembers everything wrong. When he left the first time, when he was twenty, I begged him to take me with him. I said, *please* don't leave me with Them. I bet you didn't know what a horror show my parents were."

I'm so sorry, Cindy thought. *I didn't know. I didn't know.*

"He says he came back for me the next day, but he couldn't find me. What a lie. Another time he visited, I was using. He says he begged me to get clean. At least don't be a whore, he said, it breaks my heart. He was so afraid that I'd get

HIV and die. Ha. None of that happened. What I remember is he stole my stash along with my money."

And the last time, Shasta?

Cindy, who did meditate, knew how to be still.

"And nine years ago, the Grand Finale," Shasta said. "My precious brother kills the bottle, climbs on top of me, and rapes me. Rapes me, holding my wrists down and mumbling, 'My li'l sister, my li'l sister, I love you better 'n anyone.'" Tears ran down her face. "*Now* are you satisfied?"

"I'm so sorry, Shasta," Cindy said. "What happened in the morning?"

"He was gone. I never heard from him again."

"So he never knew about Daisy until you told him yesterday. How did he react?"

"He *said* he didn't believe it," Shasta said. "He acted shocked. Of course he swore he'd never do such a thing. Right, like he'd never lie or steal. He said over and over that he didn't remember and he couldn't have forgotten."

He could have. An alcoholic blackout could do that. Record button out of order. No memory, then or ever. But that was beside the point.

"He sounded so sincere," Shasta said, "that I gave in and showed him Daisy's picture. That shocked him all right."

"Aretha showed me a shot of you and Daisy on her phone," Cindy said. "She looks a lot like you."

"Not as much as she looks like Shane," Shasta said. "You said you knew him, so you don't have to trick me. Don't you lie too."

"I won't lie," Cindy said. "I agree with you. What happened when Shane saw Daisy's picture?"

"He knew. He looked at *this*!" Trembling with grief and rage, she shook her cell phone in Cindy's face. "He took one look at Daisy, and he knew."

"And what did you do to him, Shasta?" Cindy asked. "You'll feel better when you've told me."

No backup, no witnesses, she couldn't Mirandize Shasta in the Park, so what she said would be inadmissible as evidence. But she thought that once Shasta told her story, she'd come quietly.

"I felt better the moment he was dead," Shasta said, "and couldn't hurt us anymore."

* * * *

The next day marked ten years since she'd stopped drinking.

As they lay in bed that night, Bruce whispered, "You asleep?"

"Thinking."

She humped over onto her stomach and burrowed her head into his armpit. His arm tightened around her. Besides taking Shasta in to be booked yesterday, she'd had to trace the knife, mobilize a social worker she trusted to advocate for Daisy, and fill out a ton of paperwork. In a couple of days she'd be able to think about her anniversary, the love that had come pouring in when she'd told her story. It was nice to take a break from being a cop, if it didn't last too long.

Bruce's breathing quieted. He'd fallen asleep.

There's more than one good reason, she murmured, her lips against his skin. When you refuse to grow up, you don't only self-destruct. You do so much damage to the people you're supposed to love.

Elizabeth Zelvin's short stories appear in *Ellery Queen's Mystery Magazine* and *Alfred Hitchcock's Mystery Magazine, Black Cat Mystery Magazine,* and will appear in *Jewish Noir II* in 2022. Liz writes the Bruce Kohler Mysteries and the Mendoza Family Saga. She has been nominated three times each for the Derringer and the Agatha Awards. "A Breach of Trust" was listed in *The Best American Mystery Stories 2014.* Liz edited the anthologies *Me Too Short Stories* and *Where Crime Never Sleeps.*

THE MANNEQUIN GRAVEYARD

GREGORY L. NORRIS

The house where they sent Marc to hide existed at the very end of a winding dirt road. Single-lane, something not on any maps, Marc traveled over the ruts, the car barely motoring above idle, until the road ran out and he found himself facing a wall of trees. The rangy sap pines towered above him, their trunks conjuring images of prison bars.

He wondered if he'd driven far enough north to have crossed into Canada through the porous New England border. Or to somewhere at the end of the world. He hadn't cried since that ice hockey game when he was eleven, when the old man beat the tears out of him for showing emotion over the loss. A decade ago? Tears threatened for the first time since that terrible afternoon. Marc almost gave in. Then he choked them down into his guts where all the others had gone over the years. Where, he imagined, they'd turned cancerous and would eventually devour him from the inside out. Assuming, of course, he didn't get himself killed first.

He shut off the car, a ride as sweet as it was hot, and stepped out. To his surprise, his legs were shaky. He tried to blame it on the long journey—traveling to the farthest end of the planet was bound to lead to jet lag. Only he knew better. What had happened just north of the city was big—bigger than anything he'd heard of, even the infamous South Side Kings' daylight carjacking at the police station. And badder than his worst nightmare. On that point, Marc cracked what he imagined was quite the lunatic's smile. No worry about nightmares, as he didn't see himself getting much in the way of sleep going forward, no matter how safe Woody's house in the deep country was reported to be.

He stretched, shook out his feet, and started through the prison-bar wall of tall pines. The air was narcotic in its lush greenness—pinesap, the remote forest, fallen needles and leaves, all of it cooking in the summer's humidity. A note of smoke turned him in the right direction, toward a break in the green and the small house nearly concealed by the forest. Something buzzed close to his ear. Marc swatted at the offender and hastened forward.

The house pulled free of the trees and renounced its camouflage. At first glimpse, he hadn't thought the place more than a shack, likely a kind of hunting camp. But as he neared, that observation proved false, likely one more aspect of the house's disguise. It was a single story place, the exterior weathered gray natural siding, with windows and doors and a peaked roof. A curlicue of smoke in the shape of a question mark drifted up from one corner behind the house along with the melody of a song he could almost place, performed through a man's whistling. Marc's pulse quickened for reasons he couldn't identify. For days, his heartbeat had run in a gallop. He rounded the corner of the house and caught his first smell of the thick steaks on the grill and stole a look through the oily gray smoke at his host and savior, Norman L. Woodard.

"Woody?" Marc asked.

Woody stood dressed in jeans cut into shorts with plenty of strings showing, an old T-shirt with a rip under one arm, and a green apron upon which were words urging someone, anyone, to kiss the cook. He was an older man, thin, with a shock of gray hair pulled into a ponytail. He smiled, and relief flooded through Marc. But after a second of staring at Woody's welcoming smile, another sensation superimposed over his relief—fear.

"And you must be the major league fuck-up who fucked up major league big time," Woody said.

"Guilty," Marc said.

And was he ever.

* * * *

Steaks and potatoes wrapped in foil, baked on the grill, and ice-cold beer followed. They sat outside on a patio made from brick pavers in old Adirondack chairs that had been there so long the paint had worn off, leaving indestructible gray wood miserable on the ass and spine.

"It's bad," Woody said. "A real shitstorm. I'm not gonna lie."

Marc ate, forcing down the meal, his stomach filling up with shards of broken glass and angry wasps. He imagined the cancer spreading beyond the soft lining of his gut, metastasizing into his blood stream and other tender organs.

"A cop, dude. Bad enough you dragged him. But after he croaked in the hospital, well that's a whole different level of fucked-up-beyond-all-recognition."

Fresh sweat ignited across Marc's forehead. He pressed the cold, damp barrel of his longneck against his temples but the connection only made him feel hotter. "Tell me something I don't already know."

Woody belched and eyed him.

"No, seriously," Marc said. "Tell me."

Woody shrugged and flashed the sparest of grins, the gesture more wolf's snarl than actual smile. "I don't know. You're here, and for now that means you're off the grid. What happens next is anyone's guess. As has already been stated, you're *fubared.*"

Silence fell over the patio along with the lengthening shadows. From somewhere among the trees came the melancholy song of a mourning dove.

"Until we do know the next move, you're here. You'll have a room, three squares, and all the time in the world to ponder the meaning of life. And when you get sick of that—" Woody raised his beer bottle and tipped its neck at the trees, pointing into the woods. "I'll show you something up there I discovered when they first set me up here. Something as fucked as you, kid. Mind-blowing in its fucked-up-ness. One of those things that, once you've seen it, can't be unseen."

A chill teased the fine hairs at the nape of Marc's neck. He fought it, failed. The shiver tumbled down his backbone. "What kind of thing?"

"The old town dump up in the woods. Yeah, there used to be something of a town here. It's gone for the most part but the dump isn't," Woody said. "Something they left there years ago."

Marc shrugged. Woody took another pull, exhaled, and smiled.

"I call it the mannequin graveyard."

* * * *

Pondering his life wasn't any more successful than sleep. The best Marc managed of the latter was to drift into a fugue state between sleep and the waking world, hypnotized by the constant background song of night insects through the window screens.

The house had bottled the heat and exuded a smell of old socks and the multitude of older books that lined shelves in the front room. The bed was comfortable enough, he supposed. The room contained a men's bureau, antique and made from solid wood. Its drawers were stuffed full of clothes and a few oddities, like foreign coins in a catchall among the changes of underwear, and a little jade Buddha head.

In the darkness, he imagined himself at the bottom of a well. Worse, in Hell, Hades—whatever the place was called. Not knowing, not sleeping, was his eternal punishment for a young life soaked in sin and, now, blood. Not that he'd believed much of that religious mumbo-jumbo after his eleventh winter.

Sighing, Marc rolled over. He wondered how many other fubared members of the South Side Kings had tossed and turned in this very bed before him, sweating and taking stock of their lives. How many tears, how much nervous sweat, had the mattress absorbed? How many of his fellow lost souls had Woody taken into the woods to see something that, once seen, couldn't be unseen?

"The mannequin graveyard," he whispered.

Saying the words made sleep even more elusive.

* * * *

He drifted off only to jolt awake, his full bladder conspiring against him. Sounds from the kitchen drew Marc down the throat of the house, whose windows gazed out at the endless green. Woody stood at the stove, which ran on bottled gas, flipping eggs in a frying pan. He was naked apart from his cook's apron.

"You're up."

"Yeah. Is there coffee?"

Woody aimed the spatula toward the French press standing on a length of open counter. "Help yourself. You want some breakfast?"

"Sure. Along with a side order of you putting on pants."

Woody looked down at his nakedness. "Oh, yeah. Been a while since I had company."

He shifted the skillet off the flame, killed the burner, and headed down the hallway to the other of the two rooms at the back of the house.

The robust brew went down well and helped Marc to focus. Woody emerged dressed in the same jean cut-offs and apron.

"You hear anything from above?" Marc asked.

"Just the birds. To answer your question, not yet. As soon as I do, you'll know it."

"Where do they usually get sent?"

Woody picked up his coffee cup and wrapped his long, thin fingers around the bowl. "They?"

"The ones who come to your safe house. After, is it Canada or Mexico?"

Woody leaned his hip against the counter. "Canada or Mexico, sure."

"Because I'm sick of the winters. And I wouldn't mind hiking through the jungle, especially with a flock of hot *senoritas.*"

Woody raised his cup in a toast. Again, that wolfish snarl-smile spread across his thin lips. Even then, Marc knew it was a lie. Mexico. Anywhere after the safe house. That the house was safe. All of it.

"I've been thinking," Marc said.

"You probably shouldn't do too much of that."

He ignored the weight of Woody's comment. "That place in the woods you told me about."

The snarl flattened off Woody's face.

"I want to see it."

* * * *

It started to rain, not the sort of soaking downpour that would stamp out the humidity but one of those trickles designed to stoke it. A hollow plunking as drops struck leaves followed them up a rise, where they picked up part of an abandoned fire road through the stands of pine, oak, maple, and white birch, along a length of farmer's wall, and to a place deep in the woods where the trees grew so close together that their canopy nearly blocked the sky.

"The old town dump," Woody said. "It's not far ahead."

They hiked onward. The trail bottomed out in a hollow filled with perfumed wildflowers buzzing with bees and picked up ahead. To the right, under a hedge of poison oak whose crowns spilled with toxic red-velvet petals was an additional oddity. Several cars sat abandoned in that corner of the woods. All of the wrecks had been stripped and torched. The moisture drained from Marc's mouth. Those other guests before him. Now he knew the truth. End of the world. End of the line. It was all pretty much the same when they sent you here.

Tense, he walked on, Woody a step ahead.

"I found it up here," Woody said, shattering the spell of thoughts he'd fallen prey to. "Damndest thing."

The cars were at their six now. Ahead, beyond a length of lichen-encrusted stone wall, rose a jumble of body parts—arms, legs, torsos, and heads. One nude woman jutted armless from the trunk of a pine like an old figurehead on a clipper ship. No optical illusion, the curiosity was sprouted from the tree's hide.

"How—?" he stammered, suddenly struggling to breathe.

"Ain't that something?" Woody chuckled. "The tree grew around it, absorbed the damned mannequin into itself. Tells you how long this place has been around."

He'd started to suspect, given what he already sensed was coming, that the mannequin graveyard was a euphemism for Woody's killing place. But no, the graveyard was real. A real graveyard of plastic in the shape of people. Vacant eyes, most like the Adirondack chairs missing paint, tracked them as they neared.

"It creeps me the fuck out," Woody said.

Marc swallowed and nearly gagged on the dryness sitting atop his tongue. "Why?"

"You mean beyond the obvious reasons?" Woody laughed, but the sound lacked all humor. "It's a reminder."

"Of what?"

"That we're all mannequins, all *marionettes* from the time we come into this world. Flesh becomes plastic, and someone's always pulling our strings. We're all puppets, all slaves to something."

Steeling himself, Marc faced the mannequin graveyard and waited for the killing blow. Woody's words echoed through his thoughts, the last he would ever hear.

"We sure are," he said and closed his eyes.

The next few seconds tolled with the weight of minutes, hours. He hoped it would be quick. What felt like weeks, years later, he opened his eyes. Woody stood at the tree with the mannequin figurehead, relieving himself on its trunk. An acrid whiff of urine stung at his nostrils when he was able to draw in breath.

"There, now you've seen it," Woody said while zipping up. "Ready to head back?"

Cold slithered over Marc's skin. "No, I think I want to stay here a little longer."

Woody studied him, the snarl back on his mouth. "Here?"

"Yeah, by myself if you don't mind."

"I don't mind," Woody said. "Think you can find your way back?"

"Sure. If not, well, I'm not your problem anymore, right?"

Their eyes connected, and in that bottled gaze Marc caught Woody's true intentions. He'd dodged death in the mannequin graveyard but only because this wasn't where Woody took out his unsuspecting targets. The ground was too hard, too full of roots, to bury a body here. This graveyard was only for mannequins.

"Suit yourself," Woody said.

Marc nodded. Woody turned and ambled away, whistling a tune, leaving him alone with an untold number of the plastic dead.

* * * *

The patter of rain added to his sense of isolation, and a low breeze gossiped through the graveyard, stirring the raw scent of earth and summer green.

Marc's gaze drifted over the piles of bodies and limbs sprouted from decades of fallen and rotting needles. His life was over, that much he already knew. It had ended because of that wrong turn following a wrong decision. The cop held on. Marc accelerated, dragging him for half a mile. What got shipped to the hospital, according to the little he'd heard, hadn't lived long.

Woody was right. He was as much a puppet, a mannequin, as the things scattered before him, dumped deep in the woods, used, abandoned, and forgotten. They wouldn't let him escape this place. The steaks, Woody's hospitality, all of it was leading up to his demise. Last suppers in preparation for final breaths.

The sough of the wind cooled his sweat. The mannequins stared through dead eyes. Emotion washed over him, and for the first time since the afternoon of the hockey game, Marc cried.

The tears poured out of him, fat and saline. His breath hitched with sobs. The energy fled his legs, and he dropped to his knees on the fragrant carpet of rotting pine needles. By the time he again stood, he'd been there so long that the storm had worsened, the day darkened, and his muscles ached.

Flesh becomes plastic, he thought.

* * * *

Woody entered the dark bedroom.

"I'm so sorry, kid," he whispered, and Marc believed him.

The older man moved with grace and agility, like a shadow, over to the bed. There, he thrust the blade into a patch of bare back showing from the bunched sheet. Steel struck plastic.

"What the fuck—?" Woody gasped.

Marc moved out of cover from his crouch beside the men's bureau and was on him lightning-fast. Woody howled as the knife hit target. And then, as he fell onto the mattress, he laughed.

"You were right," Marc said. "Once seen, I couldn't un-see it."

Woody started to answer. What emerged was gibberish, dying words soaked in blood.

* * * *

He fixed coffee in the French press and drank it.

"Not bad," Marc said to the empty house.

He found Woody's cell phone. No messages had come in since before Marc's arrival, no new plans for the Kings' worst problem, no trips to Mexico or Canada. The only solution had been ordered from the start. Marc dropped the phone, lit the match. While the small house in the deep woods burned, he set off for the mannequin graveyard.

What felt like hours passed. He walked, the forest blurring around him, the way ahead not always clear. Long after setting out, he found himself standing in front of the graveyard, staring into the tangle of limbs and faces.

Saying nothing, Marc stripped. Naked, he wandered into the mannequin graveyard and sat among the pieces. Then, closing his eyes, he surrendered.

Gregory L. Norris writes for national magazines, short story anthologies, novels, and the occasional episode for TV and film. His modern noir feature film screenplay *Amandine* was optioned in 2020 by a Hollywood production company. He writes the *Gerry Anderson's The Day After Tomorrow: Into Infinity* novels for Anderson Entertainment in the U.K., and his time travel romance, *Ex Marks the Spot,* releases from Woodhall Press in September 2021.

SAVING THE *INDIANA DAE*

VICKI WEISFELD

When Bruce Pritchard unlocked the door to his quirky weekend getaway spot in Cape May, New Jersey, one Friday early in June, the wind crowded in behind him, gusts of rain snapping at his heels. He flipped the light switch and shed the old-fashioned boots, oilskins, and sou'wester he affected, a fully wired city boy summoning the crusty New England sea captains of his imagination.

He lit the fireplace to exorcise the weekday shadows and dispel the ocean's powerful breath, which swirled about him like a salt-tinged mist. In the kitchen, he unpacked provisions—steaks and Idahos for friends on Saturday, a purple-black cluster of mussels for tonight, a bottle of pinot grigio, ditto. This he opened eagerly, after a prolonged search found the corkscrew hiding among the dish-towels.

He toured his strange dwelling, created from the hull of the once-derelict schooner *Indiana Dae*, buoyed by its oddities. In the late 1800s, the storm surge of a powerful hurricane propelled her up one of the Cape May Inlet's many short arms. She came to rest some fifty yards above the high tide line. When the locals first saw her there, so erect, she appeared to be still floating serenely on the water, but she'd run aground on a sandbar that was clearly visible once the storm waters retreated. The townspeople expected to see her captain treading the deck in frustration. But the *Indiana Dae*'s captain and most of its crew were lost, blown overboard and washed out to sea.

The rise of steamships had already made the *Indiana Dae* an anachronism, putting a foreseeable end to her days afloat. Quite miraculously, she was only slightly damaged in her unanticipated detour to this sandy drydock. Once sta-bilized, she put in a good many decades as a tourist attraction, though since the 1960s, she had been virtually abandoned.

Bruce bought her from two elderly sisters divesting themselves of an accu-mulation of properties as they made the transition to assisted living. *Not a moment too soon,* he thought, judging by their rambling conversations and the ship's deterioration. They'd used the *Indiana Dae* as an occasional retreat, but the condition of the ship and of the sisters had made that too dangerous for some time. "A derelict," the sisters' lawyer muttered. "A lost cause." His skepticism only hardened Bruce's determination to bring her back to life.

This weekend would be a celebration. His renovations were finally, finally finished, and the *Indiana Dae* was beautiful. The next evening his six best friends—and investment clients—were driving down from New York to enjoy his charming, freshly varnished gem.

Tonight's storm marked the end of a hot, humid spell, and by the next evening delightfully clear weather was expected. *Indiana Dae*'s top deck would be a perfect mix-and-mingle area. He'd have all his binoculars on deck for the shore bird fans. He planned to set up the bar on the quarterdeck. That reminded him: he'd have to find the box of new wine glasses that wasn't where he remembered putting it.

If the evening grew chilly, his guests could descend the ladder to the room he called the saloon. It encompassed the entire main deck, including the former captain's quarters and a feature peculiar to the ship's now-landlocked status, a fireplace. The saloon's bow end, nearest the revamped kitchen, served as a dining room. The original galley had been little more than a closet, though it served a full complement of sailors for decades. The "new galley" was six times its size and roomier than the kitchen in Bruce's Manhattan apartment.

He walked aft to the wall of windows looking toward the rain-grayed sea and the onset of evening, glass of wine in hand, shedding the week's Wall Street frustrations like a sodden overcoat. The captain must have stood in that same spot many times, watching how the ship's wake marked her passage. He sniffed the air. *Something ... what is it? Pipe smoke.* Maybe the damp air had teased a hundred and forty-year-old smell from those aged timbers. Was that possible? He took pleasure in the thought that the ship's captain—the master of the *Indiana Dae*—might have left these smoky traces.

A line of sand-clouded puddles ran across the new hardwood planking, from the base of the ladder to the fireplace, disturbing the perfection of the moment. Bruce chided himself as he fetched a towel to dry them. He must have tracked in water, but when? He'd come in the front door, climbed the few steps inside and walked straight to the galley. Plus, he remembered wiping his feet. Or thought he did. *You're losing it, buddy. First the wine glasses, now this. No, first the corkscrew, then the wine glasses, now this. You've been working too hard. You need a break.*

After dinner, he sat in front of the fire and paged through a musty volume of nautical prints—oversized engravings of merchant ships, three-masted clippers, an artist's impression of the legendary *Flying Dutchman*. Sea lore contained so many ghosts. *Why is that?* Maybe because ships so often disappeared when they were out of anyone's sight. With cell phones recording every moment and GPS tracking ships' movements around the globe and modern weather forecasting, the unknown was evaporating fast. He liked those saltwater-drenched ghosts, and muttered lines from "The Phantom Ship":

A ship sailed from New Haven
And the keen and frosty airs,
That filled her sails at parting,
Were heavy with good men's prayers.

* * * *

In his ear, so clearly he whipped his head around to see who stood behind him, he heard a rasping whisper, "Lamberton."

Lamberton? Who the hell is he? Or is it a ship's name?

The book of engravings had an index and, yes, George Lamberton was in it. He was captain of a great ship on which the New Haven colony's fortunes depended, but it was lost at sea. The lines Bruce had uttered from Longfellow's poem were about that ship's fate. That was a legend he hadn't known.

He'd found the book in a cabin on the level below the saloon. The batty sisters had used it for storage. It had been a farrago of yellowing volumes, stacks of framed pictures, half-empty chests, and broken whatnots. The sisters told him they never went inside and gave him a sly look.

"Noises," one said, "best not to be too curious."

"Or disturb things," said the other.

Such a potential treasure trove made Bruce curious, and one of the first tasks he set himself was clearing it out. It carried the smell of goods locked up too long. Completely contrary to the sisters' advice, he propped the small room's door open to air it out. Nothing inside appeared to have particular value, but the owner of an antique junque store in town eagerly bought several pieces. Bruce kept a battered sea chest, which he placed at the end of the corridor, installed a glass shelf above it, and had the electrician light it with a spotlight. "S. Newsome" was stenciled on the top. Inside were the owner's clothing, navigation tools, and medical kit. All this he left as it was.

Deep into the night before the party, the parting gusts of the ocean storm provided a soundtrack for dreams of howling seas and wind-battered sailors, decks slippery as glass, whiplashing ropes and splitting sails. Though Bruce awoke to bright sunshine, he felt as if he'd tussled with the elements for hours. The bedroom porthole revealed the morning light chasing the ocean waves, at low tide, a quarter-mile away. His prize view. He never tired of it.

He was pouring his first cup of coffee when Mary Benaker's station wagon pulled into the smoothed patch of sand next to his BMW. He threw on a robe and met her at the door. Mary was the real estate agent who kept an eye on the place for him, arranged his cleaning service, and oversaw any weekday workmen. Bruce found her tiresome, but he couldn't deny she'd been a godsend during the renovation. No slapdash repairs with Mary on the case. For eighteen harrowing months. Now she held a flat of colorful annuals.

"Thought you might want these," she said, too cheerful for the hour and him with barely any caffeine in his system. "I just drove past the farmers market. They've got strawberries."

Bruce regarded the banal mix of orange marigolds, red salvia, and purple-and-white petunias. Nothing he would plant. Certainly not in that color combination. "No thanks. I'm headed to the garden center today myself. Very kind of you, Mary, but, no."

She gave the rejected flowers a wan look and said nothing.

As an afterthought, he said, "One thing, though. Was the maid service here last week?"

"Next week. First and third Wednesdays. Everything OK?"

He looked past her, head cocked. "Yes, but...." He paused to focus a thought. "Everything looks moved, slightly, like someone dusted. And, it just feels like ... someone's been here." These weren't the only unsettling feelings he'd experienced during his previous few weekend visits. But he wasn't planning to tell Mary about the creepiest of them, the feeling someone was watching him. That sensation he chalked up to urban paranoia and, possibly, too much cabernet.

Now she hesitated. "Anything missing?"

"Nothing like that. Probably my imagination." He wished his voice conveyed more confidence. "Thanks, anyway." He indicated the plants.

"Suit yourself," she said, opening the tailgate of her station wagon and setting the plants inside.

Bruce leaned against the door frame, mildly annoyed, as she drove away. Throughout the endless renovation, she managed to slip a little dig into every conversation. "If that's what you like," "Of course, that's up to you," "I'm sure you know best." Her dislike for his choices, his polished style, couldn't be clearer. "Suit yourself" was her favorite.

"So what!" he scolded himself, closing the front door. From there, he could climb a half-dozen steps to the saloon level, or descend the same number to the sleeping cabins. He went up, and entering the saloon, he took a stumbling step forward, then another, transfixed by what he saw over the fireplace. In the place of his prized large-format Robert Mapplethorpe photograph—two male torsos, one black, one white, so rich in tone it seemed a color print, but wasn't—sailed a Baltimore clipper, sheets unfurled and running with the wind straight toward him, an old-fashioned image right out of Currier & Ives.

He wheeled and raced up the ladder to the top deck. "Mary!" he shouted, but the retreating station wagon turned onto the road and disappeared behind a stand of beach plums.

The frame of the Mapplethorpe peeked above the back of one of the saloon's low sofas. He pulled it from its hiding place and marched to the fireplace to switch the two artworks, if *artwork* is what you could call such a sentimental and clichéd sea-painting. He took a step back to admire the change and stepped in a puddle of seawater containing a miniature beach of sand and a thread of seaweed. *Is there a leak?* Craning his neck to inspect the beamed ceiling, he certainly couldn't see any sign of one.

He'd investigate after he showered. Maybe the water would clear his head. He poked his head into the guest bathroom, to make sure it was ready for company. Unfamiliar scrimshaw ornaments cluttered the glass shelf over the sink. Where had these come from? *Cheap plastic souvenirs, someone's idea of a joke.* He gathered them up to toss into the trash, but their weight, the detail, fine cracks, a map he recognized as Nantucket Island, and the date—1846—gave him pause. He set them back on the glass. *Housewarming present?*

* * * *

An hour later, piece of toast in one hand and smartphone in the other, he called Mary. "Who lived here before the old ladies' family owned the place, do you know?"

"Let me ask Chuck. If he doesn't have the answer, he can find out." Chuck Benaker was her husband, another realtor and a past president of the county historical society. These combined interests could generate a dizzying amount of genealogical detail about any parcel of local property. Bruce found Chuck even more tiresome than Mary, but she was right. He would know.

Bruce was planting herbs in his side yard when Mary called back.

"Chuck says the *Indiana Dae* was originally owned by her captain. This would have been up until he died in the storm that forced the ship aground. About 1880. The family whose property it came to rest on kept it as a tourist attraction for a couple of generations. Then in the sixties we had several big storms, and the owner sold his New Jersey property and moved to Florida.

"A real estate speculator bought the land. He was an absentee owner. But somebody along the way made enough repairs to keep the ship in reasonable condition. After he died, his widow wasn't interested, and eventually she left it to a couple of nieces—the sisters you bought it from. It deteriorated pretty fast after that."

"When I bought it, it had been abandoned so long, it was a safety hazard."

"Very good of you to take on that derelict, Chuck says."

"It hasn't gone through that many hands, considering."

"No, it hasn't. Where it landed, it's kind of tucked away, and being ashore, it's no hazard to navigation, which would worry the Coast Guard. I think people just forgot about it. The sisters were lucky. If it was high on anybody's radar, they could have been hit with a monster insurance bill."

"Tell me about it. What does Chuck know about the ship's captain?"

"He said the historical society has some papers and such. They open for the season in a couple of weeks, but wait." Mary put her hand over the receiver and spoke to someone. "Chuck says he can meet you there about three today, if you'd like."

* * * *

The Cape May historical society headquarters and museum occupied a simple clapboard house on Washington Street. Chuck Benaker looked up from a pile of unopened mail. "So, the *Indiana Dae*? Quite a history." He handed Bruce a folder. "Captain Newsome was a true legend."

"S. Newsome?" Bruce asked, remembering the stenciling on the trunk.

"Samuel. That folder has the original transfer of ownership of the ship to the owner of the property where it ran aground—a tourist trap operator a century ago and then some. He let people visit the boat while they waited for the horse-drawn trolley tours he ran from the site. Some other documents too. Papers found after Newsome was murdered, I suppose."

"Murdered?"

"Newsome? Oh, yeah. Made enemies like Dunkin' makes Donuts. If he hadn't died, he probably would have been charged with a murder or two himself. Beat the rap by bleeding to death out in the ocean. The clippings are here somewhere." Chuck walked to a file cabinet and rattled a drawer open. "We've been closed since the season ended, and the girls left everything a mess." He slammed the drawer. "But I remember the story."

Bruce leafed through the folder, mesmerized. So much for his home as peaceful retreat, a refuge. He held up a green feather.

"Ah. Newsome's parrot, 'Cap'n,'" Chuck said. "According to their diaries, the Cape May ladies were more terrified of Cap'n than of Newsome himself. Stunning vocabulary. Anyhow, Newsome sailed out of East Coast ports from Massachusetts to Savannah."

Bruce could see the rest of the afternoon unwinding drearily in front of him, despite Chuck's colorful rendition of the tale.

"Oddly," Chuck continued, "the murder didn't happen in the captain's quarters. There was a huge storm, and he'd gone down the ladder into the hold for some reason, we'll never know why, to where the cabins are today." He pulled out a schematic of Bruce's renovation and pointed to his bedroom, the largest of the below-decks cabins. "That's where it happened. When I unearth the newspaper stories, you can read the police description. Strong stomach?" He looked at Bruce over the top of his half-glasses.

"That's where I sleep," Bruce said, staring at Chuck's tapping finger.

"Really." Chuck paused, as if he found that fact significant, and the word hung ambiguously in the air. "Newsome and his killer, Henry Carver—now there was a prophetic name—had a royal feud about ownership of the *Indiana Dae*. Newsome thought Carver was a cheat. Never could stand a cheater, apparently. Came to a head one night, in the middle of a screaming storm, both of them drunk. Newsome struggled up to the top deck, maybe looking for help, but him and most of the rest of the crew were lost.

"The police got the story from a couple of deck hands who managed to survive. Carver stayed below and made it to shore after she beached. He tried to escape across the Pine Barrens, but a timber rattler got him, so the police said."

Bruce caught the skepticism. "You don't believe it?"

Benaker shrugged. "Folks in town didn't believe it. The night in question, one of the survivors said Newsome's last words were, 'I'll come back and get you.' That's how Carver died, people figured."

"What time is it?" Bruce said, as if wakened from a bad dream, and checked his watch: four-thirty.

"Oh. Sorry to keep you." Chuck looked disappointed. "I get all wound up in these stories. Cape May County has a colorful history, that's for sure."

Bruce stood up, wobbly from information overload. Mary had glossed over the tale of bloody murder. She probably thought it didn't make a good sales pitch. "No, it was … fascinating. But I have friends coming at seven."

"You go on. When I dig up those clippings, we can talk again." Chuck rubbed his hands together, a gesture whose eagerness made Bruce wince.

Back at the *Indiana Dae*, the windjammer print was above the fireplace again. This time the Mapplethorpe had been torn in half and pitched into the trash barrel outside, frame and glass shattered.

* * * *

Bruce's guests thought the renovated *Indiana Dae* was absolutely fantastic and regarded the Baltimore clipper as an inspired bit of camp. But their enthusiasm didn't improve their host's mood, and he had to force himself to be convivial. His mind was full of questions and speculations he couldn't talk to his New York friends about. He couldn't sound so unhinged—*ghosts? murderous ones?*—and expect them to invest their life savings with him.

Down the steps from the saloon level, five cabins with bunk beds had been built into what had been the ship's hold. He showed his overnight guests where he stored extra blankets and how to open the portholes. No need for instruction on how to use the head—the renovation included two modern bathrooms on the cabin level, one decorated with scrimshaw, possibly fake.

Bruce planned to sleep on a pull-out couch in the saloon, the better to keep an eye on things. Once all was quiet below, he lay awake for hours, despite his confidence that a sunny Sunday morning at the beach would expunge Newsome's gory phantom.

Too soon he was awakened by a commotion in the kitchen, as his visitors prowled for coffee. They clustered around the dining table, staring at a tall bell-shaped object covered with a fitted cloth.

"Looks like my mother's mixer," said one, "only bigger."

"Your mother dressed her appliances too? I thought that was my mom's Midwestern chic."

Bruce guessed what the thing was. But he lifted the cover, anyway.

"Cap'n's back," squawked the parrot, followed by an outpouring of dark obscenities.

* * * *

Late that afternoon Bruce phoned the Benaker real estate office, and Chuck picked up.

"Hey, Bruce," Chuck said. "Haven't found those newspaper articles yet."

Bruce interrupted his realtor's husband, told him about his desire to sell the *Indiana Dae* despite his brief ownership, and explained why.

He was grateful, a few weeks later, that the Benakers made getting out of his hasty purchase so easy. He took a bit of a financial bath on the renovations, but the advantage of quick action almost made up for that. He worked in investments. He knew about losses and could weather this one.

Greater than the financial setback was the blow to his spirit. He'd loved the schooner, the curving bulkhead walls, drinks on the top deck watching evening creep over the water. And Cape May was fun and funky, with its beautifully maintained Victorian houses—the painted ladies—its fish joints and upscale restaurants and gift shops. During spring and fall, millions of birds migrated through the area, making it a prime bird-watching spot. He missed it. All of it. So one Saturday in mid-August, he made a reservation at one of the fancy B&Bs and drove the two and half hours south once again.

He hadn't planned to revisit the *Indiana Dae*, steering clear of a potential swamp of nostalgia, but he couldn't help himself. He wondered whether the Benakers had found a buyer yet. His chest tightened the moment she hove into view. The lines of colorful pennants he'd put up, *at considerable risk to life and limb*, flapped from the yardarms. He saw lights and, not wanting to intrude on the apparent new owners, parked about a block away amidst a small fleet of cars. Birdwatchers, judging by their bumper stickers.

There was no "for sale" sign at the ship; maybe it had been a quick turn-around. Through the windshield, he watched the sea view he'd loved, and let the movement of the waves relax him.

He hadn't been parked more than a few minutes before Mary Benaker's station wagon whizzed past and turned into the sandy parking area next to the ship. *Open House? Checking to see whether she's ready for a potential buyer?*

Those were reasonable theories until Mary opened her tailgate and grabbed two heavy bags of groceries. Bruce grabbed a pair of bird-watching binoculars. Mary fumbled at the door, setting the bags down alongside a garden of spindly red and orange and purple flowers newly planted where his herbs had been.

"OMG," he said. "*She wanted Indiana Dae.*" It came to him then how careless Mary had been about keys, especially for a realtor. It took forever for her to get the keys from the sisters, and Mary never gave him her key after the renovations were finished. That was so she could let in the maid service, she'd said.

Mary could have sneaked in and put up that godawful painting. It made him angry all over again to recall the destruction of the Mapplethorpe. She had all week to move things ever-so-slightly, to hide things, to display scrimshaw, to hide his new wine glasses. He was in Manhattan; how the hell would he know what she was up to? Then Chuck with his tales of murder and retribution. Were they true, or had he been duped throughout? Chuck never had produced those elusive newspaper clippings. And, come to think of it, why did Chuck have a copy of the *Indiana Dae*'s renovation plan right there in his office? Bruce could kick himself. If only he'd thought to get a nanny-cam before his precipitous decision to sell.

The Benakers' possible duplicity didn't account for everything, though. Some things occurred while he was present. The parrot. That wasn't explained. The puddles of seawater. True, Mary could have left those. The pipe smoke. Was that his imagination?

Bruce drummed the steering wheel. As twilight came on, the saloon lights glowed yellow against the sky's deepening blue. He raised the binoculars. Mary crossed to the windows, a glass of red wine in her hand, as if she owned the place.

No doubt she does.

He drove to the B&B and took a long walk, trying to throw off some of his anger. *A nice dinner and a couple glasses of wine will take the edge off.* They didn't, and the charms of the overdecorated B&B grated on him.

The next morning, he strolled to a breakfast place the locals frequented, a healthy distance from the main tourist area. He settled into a booth and ordered pancakes, poached eggs, and a crab cake. He ignored the chatter of the crowded dining room until the men in the booth behind him started loudly recounting their various run-ins with tourists—outsiders, like him—run-ins in which the locals always came out on top.

In his cigarette-roughened voice, the louder man said, "So I just played dumb and the guy figured I didn't take his meaning. So he kept on explaining, but what *he* didn't understand was I had his deposit and he could argue about it forever, but he wasn't getting it back. Meanwhile, his wife and kids are in the car, getting hotter and crankier, and he finally thinks—I could see the little wheels turning—'it's just seventy-five measly dollars. It's worth that to get the hell out of here.'"

"So he took off?" his friend asked.

"He did."

"So breakfast is on you?"

"Not hardly."

After a few minutes of clattering silverware, and the clanking of thick china mugs, the friend asked, "Whatever happened to that parrot? You must have lost money on that deal."

"Nah. I borrowed the bird. And slippery Chuck Benaker paid me plenty. The dumb old geezer comes out on top again."

Bruce's fork stopped halfway to his mouth. He could see how it all happened. And he wondered whether Mary, who was so lackadaisical about managing keys, would have had enough sense to change the locks.

* * * *

Work kept Bruce extra busy for a couple of weeks, though the *Indiana Dae* and how to get her back were never far from his mind. He made some weekend side trips to the Mystic Seaport Museum, the Philadelphia mariners' museum, and maritime museums in Annapolis and Newport News. He found photos, histories, maps—the works—including information about the *Indiana Dae* and her captain.

Instead of the irascible, possibly murderous character Chuck Benaker had described, Samuel Newsome was a well-respected figure in his day. Always described as having his pipe and tobacco pouch near at hand, he had a reputation for fair dealing and for maintaining his ship in tip-top condition.

When an indefatigable librarian handed Bruce Newsome's log and journal, a crackle of electricity coursed through him. Newsome's own words, in his own handwriting, showed he was the true owner of the *Indiana Dae*. No matter how much Bruce had paid for her, no matter his modernizations, no matter Mary Benaker's devious dealings, she was Newsome's ship. From that conclusion, a plan began to form in Bruce's mind.

Newsome had been a leader in the Seamen's Church Institute, which aimed to make seafaring safer and help the body, mind, and spirit of men far from home. He'd made a substantial donation for the construction of a chapel on Ludlam Bay, just up the coast from Cape May. If Bruce could communicate with Captain Newsome anywhere, he thought, it would be there.

What he discovered was a tiny chapel that could hold maybe five people. Bones of derelict ships formed a sort of modern sculpture garden in the surrounding yard. On the chapel's back wall hung an engraving of the "floating chapel" that once served seamen on the Delaware River. The altar was bare, except for a pair of brass candlesticks and an open Bible. In front of the altar, someone had placed fresh flowers. The ship's bell, housed in a cupola above the chapel, chimed softly as the wind off the Atlantic caught its rope.

On his first visit, Bruce sat on one of the chapel's hardback wooden chairs. He was alone, so he spoke aloud about the Benakers' betrayal. He talked about how they'd stoked his anxieties and how his growing admiration for the *Indiana Dae* contributed to his sense of loss. Those were feelings Captain Newsome would understand. If only he were there to hear them.

It was strange, but afterward, Bruce felt the load of anger and resentment he'd been carrying lighten a bit.

On his next visit, he described how they'd done it—the "misplaced" items, his Mapplethorpe photograph, the borrowed parrot. He told it as if he were speaking to a friend sitting alongside him, and he could almost believe the captain was intently listening. One thing Bruce was sure of. The captain would understand.

"They didn't just hurt me. They hurt you too, Captain. They maligned your memory, never thinking I'd figure out the truth." He took strength from the chapel's thick walls to add, "Or come here."

His third visit, a few weeks later, was in early November. The chapel was chilly. Cold from the concrete floor crept up his pants legs. He described how he hoped to reclaim the *Indiana Dae*. "Of course," he added, "I could use some help."

An hour later, as he prepared to leave, he noticed the chapel was warm. Unaware, he'd slipped off his coat as he spoke. Now he put it on again. He searched for an electronic eye that would switch on the heat for visitors, but there wasn't one. Instead, on the floor next to his feet, was a familiar puddle of sandy water trailing a strand of seaweed.

* * * *

When Bruce left the *Indiana Dae* the last time and handed Mary Benaker the key, he was consumed with sadness. He guessed that was why he'd forgotten to bring along the spare key he kept back in New York. Now that key jingled alongside the ones to his apartment and garage.

It would be wrong to say the Benakers never knew what hit them. They must have had suspicions during the few weeks Bruce made good use of that spare key. He replayed some of Mary's tricks on stealthy mid-week trips to Cape May.

Moving things, hiding them. In the middle of the night, a recording of a squawking parrot would blast from a hidden speaker, not often enough for the couple to locate the source of the noise. He dropped a green feather in the kitchen sink. Although he left the Baltimore clipper picture over the fireplace, occasionally he turned it upside down.

Perhaps it was wishful thinking, but when he found the saloon filled with the strong odor of pipe tobacco, it seemed more was going on there than his own mischief.

After those boisterous weeks, which he thought of as priming the pump, he retrieved the hidden speaker and let the Benakers' nerves work on them. From then on, he confined his Cape May visits to very public weekend trips and stays at the B&B. It used an electronic key system that recorded each time a door was opened. The Benakers might suspect him, but once he was in for the night, there was an electronic trail to prove that was right where he stayed. The B&B owners were not fans of the Benakers and delighted in recounting Mary's latest complaints, apparently a prime topic of local gossip.

She said she heard rattling noises and felt as if the ship's hull would suddenly tilt, causing her to lose her balance. *Too much wine, or is this her imagination?* It wasn't Bruce. He was in Manhattan during the week, working late, having pizza nights with friends, taking clients to dinner, his whereabouts widely known and easily verified.

In March, Bruce took a call from Chuck, who wanted to drive up to New York to talk to him. "Mary's done," he said. Bruce heard some guilt in his voice, and perhaps some hope he could cajole Bruce into admitting he was merely giving them a dose of their own medicine.

"This has gone far enough," Chuck said. "Mary's at her wits' end."

"I'm sorry she's troubled. But what do you want me to do? How can I help?"

"You can stop tormenting her."

"I'm sorry, Chuck. I haven't seen Mary since before Christmas."

"You've been coming to Cape May."

"Yes, you know how I love it. I stay at the Queen Alexandra, visit the Audubon center."

"Do you ever come out to the ship, where we, uh, live now?"

"I've put that chapter behind me. I'll be honest, Chuck. I was too hasty selling her back to you. But what seems to be the problem?"

"Did you ever … did you think … really believe, I mean … that the ship was haunted?"

"There's no such thing as ghosts, Chuck. You reminded me of that yourself." No, the stuff that had bothered him? Chuck and Mary were responsible for most of it, and rumor and his imagination did the rest. "I did smell pipe smoke occasionally, or thought I did."

"Yeah."

"And there was the unfinished cabin. The sisters used it as a storeroom."

"Why didn't you finish it? We haven't either, yet."

Bruce took a long time answering. "It's a little embarrassing. The electrician was working alone in there one day last summer, and he said the cabin was suddenly so cold he could see his breath. After a minute, he heard the water running in the new hall bathroom and called out, but no one answered. He stepped into the passage, and a large man dressed in a peacoat and cap—not summer wear, that's for sure—came out of the bathroom. Without opening the door." Bruce paused. "So he said."

"Newsome."

Bruce shrugged. "Whatever. The electrician left and wouldn't come back. The entire Cape May County electrical fraternity knew the whole story by the next morning. I decided to leave well enough alone. I didn't need the room."

"Hunh," Chuck said, staring into the space above Bruce's head. "So that's why we can't get anyone to fix our lights. They flicker."

"How frustrating."

"Did you have leaks? Puddles of seawater turning up?"

"In all honesty, no leaks."

Their dinner finished, Bruce said, "Nightcap?"

"No, thanks. I have to drive back. I can't leave Mary alone overnight."

"Sorry to hear that. Maybe her spirits will lift when the weather warms up."

"Yeah."

"Give her my best," Bruce said.

* * * *

When all was said and done, Bruce was out of his vacation home for less than a year. When he returned, he left the Baltimore clipper hanging over the fireplace and placed the sea chest in its spotlit position at the end of the hallway. First, though, he had the locks changed.

It was odd, Cape May residents said, that Bruce never made any of the complaints the Benakers had. No creepy noises in the night, no flickering lights, no rearranged closets and drawers. Though he experienced an occasional whiff of pipe smoke, at least he liked to think he did. The scent was like an old friend, following him up and down the ship's ladders. Evenings, its warm aroma accompanied him onto the top deck to watch the darkening sea.

✗

Vicki Weisfeld's short stories have appeared in *Ellery Queen's Mystery Magazine,* other leading crime fiction magazines, and various anthologies. Two stories have won top awards from the Short Mystery Fiction Society and the Public Safety Writers Association. Her blog is at www.vweisfeld.com, and she's a reviewer for the UK website crimefictionlover.com. Her first novel is under contract with Black Opal Books.

THE CONTROL TOWER
JANICE LAW

The man had been of considerable size before the coyotes and vultures. They'd left the bones and some rags of clothing but not a whole lot else.

"No one spotted him earlier?" I tried for surprise, although this was typical of the East Sector, formerly Lattonville, a hamlet specializing in cross-border commerce, legit and otherwise. With the computerized Control Towers network installed, the border was secured and the town's economy cratered, converting East Sector to a semi-criminal favela living off Tower personnel.

The local officer shrugged. Alison DeMar was wearing her usual "Fuck the Algorithm" T-shirt and her usual attitude. The cold, steady rain was not helping, either. "He'd been in a shallow grave. Animals probably unearthed the corpse. Course, out here you never know."

She gave me a significant look.

"Who found him?"

"Jimmy Higgins. Local duck hunter. Just luck."

If you could say that landing a corpse without features, identification, or obtainable prints was lucky. "I can help out with the toxicology. Otherwise—" I didn't need to say outright that she'd wasted my time on a wet night.

Her face changed. I've been around Officer DeMar often enough to read her phlegmatic expressions. That slight narrowing of her dark eyes meant that she had another card to play. "He's one of yours," she said, lifting the rags from his chest. "Suiting fabric this good and a haircut that fancy never saw Main Street. And there's this." She held up a little evidence bag with a mirrored shard.

Our tech guys are wedded to their reflective shades, so that bit of glass was suggestive. But not conclusive. "Nobody's AWOL at the moment. We're full complement and have been for months. He might have been on Special Op but more likely passing through."

Alison snorted.

To clinch the argument, I took out my scanner and ran it over the body. No beep, no light, no read out. "Satisfied?"

She bent down and shifted the corpse so that the left side of his head was visible. His left ear was missing just like his right, but no coyote had made that neat cut.

Alison looked at me. "Lotta Control Tower guys have the chip put in an ear lobe, yes?"

"Not all," I said, but I swore under my breath. A lost identity chip meant big time hassle. "I'll take him in just in case."

"Right." I got a flash of the Officer DeMar smile—maximum teeth and minimal warmth. "You can return the favor someday."

Fat chance, I thought. The less I had to do with difficult Officer DeMar the better. I'd never liked her much, and I liked her less now that she'd saddled me with a toxic problem in the shape of a mysterious John Doe.

Back at the Tower, my first stop was two levels up at the Medico's office, manned by his principal technician, a wiry, red-haired guy with a russet whisker and a fine array of tattoos, both theoretically verboten for Control Tower personnel. He was as labor averse as his boss, and his immediate line was that without a chip there was no authorization. *Authorization's* the key word with all things Tower. I contacted McKinley only to be stonewalled. "We can do DNA," I said. "We can hit the data bases and look for a match, chip or no chip."

"Theoretically," responded McKinley, but instead of authorization I received a rush order to look into recent thefts from the basement mechanicals area. Apparently, I had literally gone down in his estimation.

"What about the body? It looks as if he'd been chipped, so possibly there's an identity chip in the wrong hands."

"Anyone AWOL?"

I admitted that there was not.

"Theoretical matters are low priority," said McKinley. "Put him in storage. There is no need for us to do X-Tower police work."

Imagination is not McKinley's strong point. Everyone, me included, accepted that. As our tech bible points out, imagination more often leads to difficulties than solutions. Undeniably true, yet I couldn't help feeling that McKinley was being unusually obtuse, and after a cursory investigation of the mechanicals area, I returned to the Medic Station. There I learned that our mystery stranger had died of a head injury, most likely while comatose from drugs. I got this direct from the Medico, who, as a great concession, opened an autopsy file that revealed more about the chemicals than the trauma.

"Something quite special," the Medico said, pushing his glasses back up on this nose. "A most unusual signature. I'd imagine a very satisfactory euphoria followed by oblivion." The thick lenses magnified his eyes to give him a deceptive appearance of alertness and wisdom, but his avid expression suggested that illicit "something special" might be right up his alley.

"Can you give me some idea of the ingredients?"

He could and did. There was an opiate in the mix and something, he said, similar to certain large animal tranquilizers. "But nothing so crude, you understand."

I nodded and tapped in the details.

"We're dealing with an artist. A real pharmaceutical genius."

"My own guess was a murderer."

"Reasons?" His voice was sharp.

"The head injury you mention, the burial of the victim, and that missing ear, suggesting a stolen chip—and a potential security issue."

He looked uneasy. "A chain of assumptions," he said after a minute. "Any questions regarding Control Tower security are strictly Level One."

I must have looked unconvinced for he added, "Best leave it to McKinley. Our fate's in his hands. So to speak."

* * * *

Funny how a single incident can strike you as odd. Although I'd accepted without question that our operations would be directed by McKinley's algorithms, the whole business of John Doe unsettled me, as if I'd switched channels and nothing looked the same anymore. I discussed this phenomenon one night with Christopher, a bartender at the Fence. Relatively new, clean, and as well stocked as East Sector watering holes went, the Fence catered mostly to Tower personnel because it could be safely reached by electric cart.

The bartender nodded his head, his hooded eyes half closed. Bearded and bear-like, Christopher was a man of few words whom I found soothing and intelligent. I was set to elaborate on altered perceptions—helped along by the potent and highly sweetened local brew—when Officer DeMar came in. Surprise number one. Surprise number two: "I've been looking for you," she said. She greeted Christopher in a friendly way and asked if she could use the back room for a few minutes.

The cubical-sized annex had a window that brought in the smell of the river and of some blooming plant. A luxury of sorts; we have few accessible windows in the Control Tower. "We don't often see you here," she said.

"I am pretty well occupied with work."

She raised her eyebrows. "Yet you've been hitting the bars this week, inquiring about a variety of recreational drugs."

"You're well informed."

"I do my job."

"Would you had with John Doe last week."

She shrugged. "Surely you already know all about him. You have the resources, right? Back at that super forensic lab?"

I hesitated. In theory our cooperation with the X-Tower sectors is limited to providing technical and lab services. This had the look of a special case, where the usual parameters could be expanded. "No chip, no interest. John Doe's been cremated on authorization direct from McKinley. Plague was mentioned and anthrax is not out of the picture, either."

Alison's faced changed. We periodically have epidemic panics. "Seriously?"

"Just smoke. John Doe died of a head injury, complicated by a drug overdose."

"McKinley does smoke?"

I didn't know how to answer that so I messaged her the autopsy data. "The drug is the only lead we have left. Hence my field trips."

"Conducted," she said, "in inimitable Tower style. Every dealer in the Sector knows Security's on the case."

There was something to that, and if we'd been on better terms I would have coordinated with her department. "My problem, not yours."

"Until today," she said. "We found Henry Machado with his throat cut this afternoon. *No bueno.*"

When she added that the dead man dealt in "artisanal product," I thought immediately of the Medico's enthusiasm, but I kept my mouth shut. Though Machado was a dealer and probably a low life, he was a bona fide citizen of East Sector. It was a minor consolation for the Sector if the Tower could be blamed.

"He left young children. Perhaps you'd like to see how the other half lives and maybe supply some of that Tower sophistication."

She's a sweetie, right? But because I would undoubtedly make more of a crime scene than any X-Tower copper, I found myself at the Machado place, a weathered house with a sagging roof and a history of additions and repairs, none of them professional. A single large tree provided a patch of shade and the support for a big tire swing. There was no other sign of children.

"Church Fellowship took them in," Alison said, although I hadn't asked and didn't much care. She lifted a strip of yellow tape and unlocked a lean-to shed. Despite the gaps between the unpainted clapboards, the room emitted a strong chemical odor, plus a heavy, meaty stench centered on a maroon stain in the center of the room.

Alison waved at the litter of broken bottles, distilling equipment, upended Bunsen burners, tubing, and pipettes. The killers had been interrupted by the arrival of the school bus. "Bad scene," Alison remarked. "The driver was armed, of course. We don't take chances with the school bus and, lucky for us, Marlene's a crack shot. The killers didn't wait around."

"But they'd started breaking up the lab?"

"Right. We've been able to get samples of the chemicals and compounds, and with the autopsy information we can determine if Henry was the source."

"You have that capacity?"

A hesitation. "We had. Past tense. Henry did all our work. He was able but he was poor. He occasionally created specialized stuff, recreation for the connoisseur. Stuff no one dreamed about before the Tower."

Great. Tower personnel blamed for local artist going bad. I was about to say something snarky when I saw her expectant expression and hesitated, realizing that I didn't entirely trust our Tower lab at the moment.

"Problem?" Alison asked.

I knew a trustworthy chemist up at the county seat, and I said I'd take care of it.

Inside the main building, the furnishings were few and undesirable: a spavined couch, half dead recliners, a plain kitchen table and wooden chairs, several beds. The Machados had not been overburdened by possessions, and it did not take us long to sift through them. I saw a few children's books, a baseball bat and glove, and a plastic doll missing one arm and most of her hair. The place was slovenly except for one room with a perfectly made bed holding a small collection of stuffed animals. Alison looked at them thoughtfully but said nothing.

We checked for loose floorboards, crawled under the beds, emptied the kitchen cabinets and checked the freezer compartment of the refrigerator. We probed the eaves, explored the peak of the roof, and descended to the crawl space. After three hours we were dirty and sweaty and empty handed. As far as we could tell there was no money, no records, nothing useful.

"Did he carry cash?" I asked. "Maybe it was a robbery after all." East Sector's crime rate is off the charts.

Alison shook her head. "No, but he had access to money. He needed money for Ginny, his eldest, who has some issues. She was on the school bus, poor kid."

A sad note for sure, but nothing that advanced the investigation. A few days later, my chemist acquaintance confirmed that the unusual drug most likely came from Machado's lab. But minus the chip, I couldn't arouse interest at the Tower. When I tried to access the DNA banks, my entry was blocked, and McKinley refused to entertain questions about John Doe or his abrupt cremation. My total security focus was to be thefts from the mechanicals area, and my usual all-hours access to McKinley was sharply curtailed.

I began sliding from uneasy to paranoid, and I was in danger of becoming a regular at the Fence until the night I left the bar extra late. As I approached my electric cart, the lights went out. Not good, but not surprising, either, given the erratic power supply in the Sector.

I slid into the seat, found the switch by feel and pushed for power. Nothing. No engine, no lights. This was potentially more serious, and a motion nearby focused my anxiety. I was fumbling for my service revolver when a shot pinged off the metal framework and sent a hot pain down the side of my face. There were two men, I was sure of it, and I raised the gun, ready to risk a blind shot when a brilliant burst of white light dazzled me and panicked my attackers.

Shouts and another weapon discharged before the sound of a heavy motorbike accelerating. I hit the floor and didn't come up until someone opened the cart door. It was Officer Alison DeMar in a Kevlar vest and a surplus Control Tower helmet. I stumbled out, still half blind and deafened, blood dripping from my face. Alison shouted to one of her slacker deputies who produced a bandage and some antiseptic, then, even more welcome, another shot of the local pick me up.

"Thanks," I said when I was sitting, intact but still dizzy in the Fence. Their generator had come on and its throb matched my head.

"You do stir the pot," Alison said, her face dark.

I lifted my hands. "I was having a philosophical discussion with Christopher. Strictly off duty. And off our John Doe investigation, too."

"Well, if you're sober, you can give us a hand. Ginny Machado's gone missing. You might be useful."

Not the most enthusiastic invitation, but I'd no great desire to return to the Tower. Christopher handed me a cup of coffee, and we piled into the truck, deputies in the back. Away from the tower, East Sector was in almost total darkness; the sky, the darkest gray imaginable; the trees, coal black; the fields, rolling soot dark like some inland ocean. Not my kind of excursion territory, and I asked what time the girl had disappeared.

"Dusk," said Alison. "She waited until then, so she's headed out of town. Everyone around knows Ginny. She'd certainly have been noticed in daylight."

"So where's your tracker dog? You'll never find her otherwise."

"She'll go back to the house." Given the distance over rough ground I was doubtful, but Alison added, "She'll have no trouble. Local kids aren't scared of darkness. Besides, Ginny's special."

"You mentioned issues."

"But not the usual. Ginny's difficulty is that she forgets nothing. Literally nothing, important or trivial. The way home, pages of books, conversations, dates, names, events. Poor child, she has a burdensome gift."

We hit a particularly rough stretch, and Alison concentrated on steering, while I struggled to reconcile my throbbing head with my twitching stomach. What with mild shock and the local brew, it was several minutes before I connected the dots.

"We're not just on a humanitarian mission, I take it."

Alison gave me a glance. "We haven't found any records, no paper, nothing digital, so...."

"Daddy's little bookkeeper? Wasn't that risky?"

"Not until now. Now's another matter—especially given the attack on you tonight. Locals, they'll know her and figure the same as I have. Tower personnel, we have more time but still we best find her pronto."

Alison hit the gas, sending us rocketing over bumps and washed-out places until we reached the drive. Then she killed the lights and the engine and allowed the truck to roll quietly down the slope toward the house.

My mind was operating at half speed. "If we assume she's got the info, what's she after at the house?"

"She doesn't go anywhere without a teddy bear, and she is much attached to the collection in the house. What would you bet on? Sentiment or money?"

I remembered the menagerie in the one neat bedroom. What sort of mind would think of stashing drug profits in soft toys? But then kids are an alien species as far as I'm concerned. "How's she going to react if you show up after the loot?"

"Not well, but there's where I thought you might come in."

"Me? Do I look like Officer Friendly?"

"You look like a Control Tower functionary. And that's good, because everyone knows the Tower's involved. Ginny wants her daddy's killer caught. You're going to help."

I said that was my unofficial task. "Officially, I am on missing supplies. McKinley seems fixated on petty theft."

"McKinley's a danger. Everyone knows that except you Tower people. And he's maybe more dangerous if compromised."

"My fear exactly, though I may be becoming paranoid in the best Tower tradition."

Alison was thoughtful for a moment. She produced a pair of night goggles, another bit of Tower tech that had wandered, and began scanning the fields and the scrubby overgrown pastures. "Who's behind it?" she asked finally.

"The big unanswered question. Knowing who bought the drug that killed John Doe would be a start."

Alison abruptly held up her hand. It was a minute more before I detected motion, a small figure moving cautiously around a tumbled-down paddock to the house. Alison eased her door and I did the same. In a whisper she ordered the deputies to remain alert before we moved in.

"Ginny," she called softly when we neared the door. "Ginny, it's Alison DeMar."

We were met with a spell of deep silence before a light came on, and Alison opened the door. Ginny Machado was a small, half-grown girl with a moon face and stony eyes. She was standing in the bedroom doorway, half a dozen stuffed toys clutched in her arms. "They're mine. You've no right to them."

"Sure and you can keep them. But we'll need to examine them as part of the investigation."

Ginny gave her a scornful look. "You'll never find out who killed Daddy. Not if the Tower's involved."

"Maybe you're right," said Alison without rancor, "but this is Dave. He's Tower Security and maybe he can do something—if you're willing to help."

Despite her tender years, Ginny Machado was a skeptic. She wanted to know how I'd hurt my head and demanded my security badge. She checked my level at the Tower and asked whether I talked to McKinley.

"Most every day," I said.

"I would like to talk to McKinley," she said seriously. "I don't trust people anymore. They all lie."

This was not the time to question her trust in algorithms. I put on my best Officer Friendly voice and asked what she would say to McKinley if she got the chance.

"Wouldn't you like to know," she replied, and when Alison cleared her throat in warning, she added politely, "Mr. Dave."

"Mr. Dave needs some information," Alison said in a no-nonsense voice. "If he gets it, he can maybe identify the body by the river and find out who murdered your father. Without that information, no dice. Your choice."

She gave the child a hard stare, and Ginny's eyes filled with tears. Alison had said the girl was thirteen, but she could have passed for eleven. At last, she swallowed and nodded. "But I want all the toys. And we're to put them somewhere safe."

Alison stuck out her hand. Ginny shook it, then turned to me. Her hand was cold and very small.

"She'll be safest at the station," Alison said. "I don't want to linger here."

We stuffed the toys in a garbage bag and squeezed Ginny between us on the front seat of the truck. Back at the station, Deputy Number One was dispatched to let the Fellowship family know she was safe, while Deputy Two was stationed at the front door. Alison, Ginny, and I adjourned to a smoke-impregnated interview room. Alison found a soft drink and opened the barred windows for some air.

"You should be accompanied by a responsible adult, a guardian, or a lawyer," she told Ginny, "but if you have your dad's records—you do have them?" The girl nodded. "The fewer people who know, the better and safer for you. Understood?"

"What does Mr. Dave want?"

"Drug purchases from the last eight months."

Immediately, the child was all business. "By name or by date?"

"Real names?" I asked, not quite believing that this bedraggled moppet had serious intel.

She nodded vigorously. "Daddy knew them all. If they didn't introduce themselves right proper, he found out later. He made it his business."

Opening the possibility of blackmail, I thought, another strand in a big can of worms. "Organized by date," I said, "but I want the names and the drugs, too, if possible."

She sensed my doubt and gave me a contemptuous look. Ginny took a sip of the soda and stared into the far corner of the room. I saw her small body relax before a pause long enough for me to think, she can't, she won't, before she began in a small voice, "April nineteenth, eight forty-six p.m. Luther Strong...."

An hour later, I had recorded eight months of Henry Machado's business, and I had matched two names from the Tower. One was a janitor in the mechanicals section, whose habit might be behind the missing supplies. Wouldn't McKinley be pleased about that. The other, Zane Brecker, was a much more serious matter. He was Level One, responsible for keeping McKinley in good shape. That meant he could not only speak to McKinley, but influence him.

At this news, Alison grew reflective. "What can you learn about Brecker?"

"Everything needful if I had his DNA and access to that data base."

"Surely you could acquire a sample."

"Level One is pretty rarified. They have little contact with the rest of the Tower and they tend to pull solitary shifts. I could maybe do it but without access to the data, I'd be no further ahead."

"Is there no one you can trust to access the DNA bank?"

"The Medico has access but he's a lazy bastard, and John Doe was cremated and probably his samples are gone."

Now Alison perked up. "Not entirely. We took some and saved them. Routine procedure, in case you folks came back and said it was our problem."

I thought about this and about the Medico's delight in pharmaceutical novelties. "I can only think of one way and you may not approve."

"Try me."

"Could we get a few samples of the drug in John Doe's system, that XT-29? The Medico has a little weakness," I added.

"And in return?"

"He checks the John Doe DNA against Zane Brecker's. If they match, we have proof. If not, we're at a dead end. It's a long shot."

"No other kind out here," she said, "but who knows if there is still any in the lab. It was pretty well trashed."

"Ginny would know," I said, "wouldn't she?"

Alison smiled a trifle grimly. "Better yet, Ginny would know the formula."

* * * *

Three nights later, having dropped off the DNA sample and engaged in strenuous negotiations, I met Alison, Ginny, and the Medico in the tiny back room at the Fence. Like the policeman's, the security officer's lot is not always a happy one. I was not only about to hand a potentially toxic drug to a susceptible colleague but also contribute to the corruption of a minor. The latter, I must admit, seemed blasé about the whole business. A strange child.

The Medico had already examined the John Doe DNA, and after a few more assurances, he accessed the data base. We sat in nervous silence while he studied the lines of figures, and it seemed a long time before he said, "You were correct. John Doe was the real Zane Brecker."

"How is it that ringer didn't amend his file?" Alison asked. "Since he was able to block Dave from the data bases?"

The Medico shrugged. "Any update of medical or genetic data would have to go through me, so best not to get fancy. But who knows," the Medico said with a sigh, "human stupidity knows no bounds. Perhaps he just figured that Brecker's body would never be found."

He tapped his fingers on the table impatiently, and Alison nodded to Ginny. "You'll want to record this, I'm sure," she told the Medico.

His pad was out in an instant, and as Ginny recited the formula and detailed the process, he tapped away. "There are exactly four samples left," she said when she was finished and passed over a tiny envelope. These are half dose. Daddy was always very careful with his clients. Mr. Brecker must have been careless."

The Medico's large fleshy hand shot out, and the packet disappeared into his breast pocket. "I'll be going," he said.

"We'll come with you."

He hesitated and began excuses that I didn't entirely trust. "Alison needs to make the arrest," I said. "The crime began in East Sector, so she's involved. Think of some good reason for her admittance. I don't want anyone getting a warning."

The Medico pursed his lips and frowned, but when we reached security, he spun a fine yarn about a new anthrax med that was urgently needed in East Sector, and once we were inside, he told McKinley that he was sending me and an East Sector medical colleague to Level One on an emergency health code.

I heard him say "possible anthrax exposure" as Alison and I hustled to the elevator. With the temporary code, we were admitted to Level One, the nerve center of the tower, a world with soft lighting, a bank of real windows, and McKinley massive and glowing in the center. The technician looked up in surprise.

"Zane Brecker?"

"That's right. Show me your authorization."

He made a move but Alison was too quick. She had cuffs on his wrists before he could touch the keyboard or switch on the mike.

"Officer DeMar is arresting you for the murder of Zane Brecker, and I am here to prevent further interference with McKinley."

The phony Brecker was a big fellow, and we had a struggle to get him into the hall and needed backup before we had him safe in the East Sector lockup. After things quieted down, I opened contact with McKinley and reported that I had solved the thefts from the mechanicals area.

"That is good," McKinley replied. "A-OK. The mechanicals area is the focus of our security concerns."

Even though he is just software, circuits, and chips, I was sorry to hear him sounding so simple minded. But not for much longer. Once we vetted all the remaining Level One technicians and ferreted out any co-conspirators, a basic reset should relieve McKinley of his obsession with petty theft and restore his trust in his chief security officer.

Should there be some other tweaks as well? I thought so. I was not as sold on the algorithms as I had been, given that the solution—and McKinley's salvation—had come from an unusual *human* mind. Though Ginny was the one person who believed wholeheartedly in his powers, there would be time enough for her to learn that no algorithm is proof against human nature.

✗

Janice Law (www.janicelaw.com) is an Edgar-nominated and a Lambda award-winning novelist, as well as short fiction writer whose stories appear in *Alfred Hitchcock's Mystery Magazine, Ellery Queen's Mystery Magazine,* and *Sherlock Holmes Mystery Magazine.* Her most recent novels are *Mornings in London* (mysteriouspress.com), and *Homeward Dove* (Wildside Press*)* and she has a story in *The Best Mystery Stories of the Year 2021.*

SLOW DOWN

STEVE LISKOW

Tiffany watched X and Y dance with the numbers and felt her racing pulse throb in her forehead. She squeezed her pencil between her fingers and forced her lips to read the problem again.

"Two X-squared minus three plus three times Y plus one equals X plus Y plus one."

Could any normal healthy person possibly give a shit? Only in algebra two, which Tiffany suspected had been invented to replace the Spanish Inquisition. Or waterboarding. Or burning bamboo slivers under her fingernails. Or the death of a thousand cuts. Or....

"Focus, damn it." She might as well tell an avalanche to stop and smell the roses. Her left foot tapped out a tattoo on the hooked rug under her desk, and she caught herself drumming in syncopation with her pencil. The Algebra Two Blues.

Slow down. Dad's voice, she could almost feel his impatience.

She forced herself to stop tapping and stamping and fidgeting, but it was hard. Ms. Brannigan spent more time breathing deeply and counting to ten answering *her* questions than for everyone else in the room combined. Maybe she could make that into another problem, one that would be more interesting and relevant than this stuff with letters and numbers that didn't have faces or names.

Oops, there she went again.

Tiff picked up the book and walked around her room, keeping her eyes on the page instead of her window overlooking the parking lot. Her walls were an almost invisible blue heather and her carpet a bluish gray so there was no abrupt transition that might distract her. Even her bedspread was in the same palette, and Mom insisted that her posters stay in the spare room.

"Two X-squared minus three plus three times Y plus one equals X plus Y plus one."

Reading out loud helped sometimes, especially if she moved, because it engaged her whole body and took up more of her attention. One of her counselors showed her that, and Mom seemed to agree. She talked to herself sometimes when *she* was thinking, too. Now that Dad lived somewhere else, they had lots of time to talk to themselves.

"OK," she coached herself. "Brackets first, then work out. Two X-squared plus six plus three Y plus three plus one equals X plus Y plus one. Subtract one from both sides and you've got...."

The numbers swirled, but she kept pacing and talking it through. Now subtract X from both sides … and then Y.…

Her hands turned slick with the effort. She hated, hated, hated algebra. She hated the classroom, no windows, and those fluorescent lights that gave everyone the skin tone of snot. Only twelve kids in the class, all the weirdos. Doreen who painted her fingernails weird colors and chewed them. She would probably die of lead poisoning. Thomas, the crack baby whose mom turned more tricks than a bridge champion to pay for her habit and passed it on to him. His mind spun its wheels like a stock car on ice. He was nineteen or twenty and still a junior they'd probably cut loose when he was twenty-one. He'd be able to vote if he could read the ballot, but he might not find the polls.

Damn, she was going walkabout again.

Tiff put down the book and ran her hands through her newly-short hair. If she solved one more problem, she could ask Mom for help. That was the deal. Mom wasn't being a bitch, she was being real. She had to know this stuff herself, even though she still couldn't figure out when she'd ever use it again.

She wanted to play guitar, which was why her guitars and her amplifier and all her music and her posters hid in the spare room. If she picked up a guitar, she'd get lost in chords and melodies for two hours instead of doing her algebra or history or English, the notes a big soft blanket around her, warm and safe. Nobody ever laughed at her when she played guitar. Those little black dots on paper talked to her like no one else ever had.

Until a few months ago.

Nigel—did anyone really have that name outside of Spinal Tap?—came up to her in the hall after American lit. His soul patch was level with her eyes and she wondered how long it took him to draw it in with eyebrow pencil. She wanted to reach up and rub to be sure it was real, but she didn't.

"Hey, Tiff," his voice smooth as the worn flannel shirt open over his Three Doors Down T-shirt. "Someone told me you play guitar really good."

"Who?" The guys loved to set her up and knock her down. She didn't admit much of anything to anyone except the kids who were as damaged as she was.

"Ben says you take lessons from the same guy he does," Nigel said. "He says you fingerpick like a son of a bitch."

Tiff remembered the first few months, struggling to build up calluses on her fingers. Her parents figured out that the guitar against her ribs soothed her more than the stuffed giraffe she'd outgrown. She hid behind that cheap Yamaha guitar, almost hid *inside* it. And the more she played, the less her fingers hurt and the more notes she could play and the taller and stronger the wall they formed.

"I guess I'm OK." She knew better than to brag. "Why?"

"Just asking." Nigel stood a head taller than she did, but probably didn't weigh as much, especially now that she was filling out and guys were noticing. She knew that was part of why they gave her grief, too.

"Some of us are trying to get something together, we don't have anyone who can play lead. Three of us can handle rhythm and a couple of us sing, but … well, you know."

"Who are the other guys?" When he told her, Ben's name was the only one she recognized. One played drums and one played bass. Nigel played keys and was kind of a geek, the poet of the school. Everyone else thought he was deep and soulful, but Tiff thought his stuff was too much about "Look at me being creative."

"Sounds cool," she said.

"Yeah, we're trying to work stuff out," Nigel said. "If you want to come around sometime, you know, jam or something...."

"Maybe. I'll let you know."

A month later, she talked to her mom about buying her an electric guitar, too.

"Are you sure, honey?" Gail Bright pulled extra hours at the hospital since Darrell, her husband and Tiffany's dad, had decided he couldn't deal with a hyper-active teenaged girl anymore. Tiff wondered if he had a girlfriend he dumped Mom for or if she herself really *did* drive him away. Mom was a nurse and tried to be a good mom. She never said it was Tiffany's fault, but she worked overtime and Tiff grappled with the algebra all by herself.

"They might let me be in a band," she said. "We might even play out a few places."

"Are any of your friends in the band?" Mom's eyes crinkled with worry. She knew how few emails and Facebook messages and texts her daughter got, most of them from the other freaky kids.

"I don't have a lot of friends, Mom." Stating the obvious. "But if I do this, maybe I'd meet more people. And I'd have fun."

Mom might not remember about fun. Since Dad left two years ago, Tiff could count Mom's dates on the frets of her guitar. She was pretty, too, eyes the color of a deep lake—forget the rings around them—hair the color of corn flakes, a laugh like wind chimes. Tiff knew she looked more like her every day. She was old enough to stay by herself if Mom had a real date, too, but what if *she* was the reason Mom didn't get out much?

Maybe "fun" touched a nerve because Mom's lips tightened.

So they went to Guitar Center and Tiff chose a Squier Stratocaster and a Fender amp small enough so she could carry it. They cost as much as four months of the Ritalin mom's health care didn't pay for. That's why she worked so much overtime at the hospital. Maybe it was why she didn't have many dates, too.

Getting used to lighter strings and more volume was harder than Tiff expected, and the pick felt slightly smaller than a dinner plate after years of fingerpicking, but she was getting there.

Now, if she could just get through this freakin' algebra. She'd removed the brackets and simplified the equation, could she factor it? Not with unknowns of different powers....

She left that problem behind and went on to the next one. Someone knocked on the door and she opened it.

Even on Saturday, her father wore pleated slacks and a tie. He had his sleeves rolled up, but he still looked like he was at work. Well, he made her feel like a job for him. That was why he left.

"When did you cut your hair?" His eyes widened, the same brown as his tasseled loafers. Two steps behind him, Mom frowned, her arms crossed and her shoulders hunched.

"A month ago." Tiff felt the tension swirl around her, a small chirping bird she forced herself not to watch.

"Hey, I couldn't make it last week. I was hoping we could go somewhere. You want to go to a movie or the mall or something?"

"And the week before that," Mom said. "You forgot the payment then, too. That's three times in a row."

"Hey, Gail, slow down, OK?" Dad turned back to her mother. "Cut me a little slack. It's been a rough month. Besides, that's going to change. I've got big news." His voice reminded Tiff of maple syrup.

"Really. The biopsy came back positive?"

"Hey, nice talk."

"Can't a girl dream?" Mom wore jeans and a sweatshirt, her Saturday cleaning outfit. "Why don't you tell me your big news, then maybe we can do something together when Tiff's finished her homework."

"I'm about half-way through the algebra and it's really hard." Tiff saw Dad smile and knew she'd made a mistake.

"Math's easy," he said. "What do I always tell you?"

"Slow down." The words felt heavy enough to crash on the living room rug.

Tiff felt herself speeding up and forced herself to feel the floor under her feet and breathe slowly.

Slow down, slow down, slow down.

She closed the door before Dad could say anything else and went back to her desk, her hands shaking. This wasn't good. It was her fault Dad left and now he was back with a big smile and big news and she thought he looked like a big dog that would bite if she stuck her hand out to pet him.

"Five X plus two Y plus seven equals...."

Dad's baritone hummed behind the door and Mom's alto answered. She sounded upset. The algebra faded and Tiff tried to make out the words. She heard "promotion" and "custody." Dad was a salesman, but whatever he was selling today, Mom wasn't buying it.

The numbers and letters whirled around the room and Tiff's heart raced after them. Her hands felt slippery and she told herself she was too old to cry.

Screw this. When the voices moved to the kitchen, she opened her door and heard a metallic thunk. Mom was boiling water for tea. She always had tea when she was upset, and now she sounded *really* upset. The refrigerator door opened and closed, then the cupboard, and a glass pinged brightly. Dad was having a beer. Mom always kept a six-pack in the fridge even though she never drank it. She and Dad were together fifteen years, some things you just get used to.

"Massachusetts?" Mom's voice rose a little higher. "Are you crazy?"

"Think about it a minute, Gail." Dad maintained his sales-pitch voice. "It's a win-win. Everybody gets something."

"You get off the hook and Tiff and I get the shaft. She's sixteen, she's making friends and getting her feet under her. She's got her music, she's busting her ass to get decent grades. And now you want to pull the rug out from under her. What kind of hare-brained—?"

"No, listen...."

Tiff felt her stomach tighten and her heart race even more.

Slow down.

She turned back down the hall to the spare room and closed the door behind her.

One wall hid behind boxes of the stuff Mom never unpacked when they moved here after the divorce. China, some blankets and towels they changed out because the closets were so small. Family pictures, the three of them so happy it made Tiff's eyes burn. A lamp, a couple of vases.

The two other walls held her posters: Mother Maybelle Carter, Memphis Minnie, Sister Rosetta Tharpe, Buffy Sainte-Marie, Joan Baez, Joni Mitchell. Facing them, Mary Chapin Carpenter, Emmylou Harris, Neko Case, Kaki King, Rory Block, Taylor Swift, and Brandy Carlisle. Her little Fender amplifier sat on the metal bookcase and her guitar case lay beside it. She unfolded the metal chair and set up her music stand on the baby-blue bathmat so the light from the window spilled on her music.

She opened her Stratocaster, pink as a stuffed animal. A girly-girl guitar, but it was cheap and it sounded good. If she played well enough, people would say a pink guitar was cool. It had lighter strings than her acoustic, and they stretched out of tune more easily. She plugged in and turned on the amplifier and clipped the tuner to her headstock, playing scales up and down the neck, hiding in the feel of the notes springing from her fingers.

Slow down. Breathe.

Pick down, up, down, up, down to the next string, up, down, up, down to the next string. Sometimes she used the pick along with a finger or two, but it messed up her picking technique, which was still almost as big a problem as equations with two unknowns.

Concentrate on the beat and the pick, she told herself. Not on the voices pounding out dissonant chords in the kitchen. She kept her eyes on the lines and dots. After five years of lessons, she could read music as easily as words. She wished algebra worked that way, too.

The voices in the kitchen grew louder and she turned her volume up a little, hiding in the scales and her picking. Down, up, down, up....

A draft ruffled the pages of her music and she turned to see Dad filling the doorframe. At least he wore the tie loose now, the knot dangling below his open collar. Mom's eyes had a look Tiff recognized from when she was five and wrote the alphabet on the living room wall with a Sharpie.

"Hey, Princess, sounding good."

Dad had a half-empty beer glass and a smile that made Tiff wipe her hands on her jeans.

"Thank you." She stood up and the guitar bumped against her chest. She wrapped her fingers around the neck and pulled it closer.

"So, let's talk about a few things, OK?"

"Like what?"

Mom leaned against the boxes near the window. She looked like the poor maid with the over-dressed rich master. But she was here all the time, working overtime, buying Tiff a guitar, helping her with her homework and listening to her when she worried about school and clothes and the boys who talked about her behind her back and called her names.

Tiffany Trank, Roxy Ritalin, Polly Prozac, Donna Downers....

"Just a few ideas," Dad said. "I've got some news and I think you'll like it."

"Make up your own mind, honey," Mom said. Her voice was low and soft and Tiff saw her straining not to yell.

She turned down the volume on her guitar and sank back in the chair. Dad moved to the wall directly in front of her so his body seemed to grow out of her music.

"OK," he said. "I was telling Mom that I've got a promotion. I'm going to be assistant director of sales for the New England region."

The sun glittered off his tie clip and Tiff forced herself to look up at his face.

"OK."

"No," he said. "You don't get what that means. It means I won't have to travel all the time. I'll have an office. And it's a big pay raise."

Mom's throat moved.

"What does that have to do with us?"

Dad scratched behind his ear. He always used to do that when he was getting into a story or a joke or a speech.

"Well, if I don't have to travel, I can spend more time at home and we can see each other more often. You could even stay with me sometimes, like weekends."

The guitar strings dug into Tiff's fingers.

"Why?"

"Well, you're growing up, and I won't have my little girl much longer. I miss you."

"That's why you didn't show up the last two weeks." Mom's words quivered.

"I got hung up on a sales deal," Dad snapped. "But that's my point. If I'm the assistant director, I won't be on the road, and stuff like that won't happen anymore."

"Where was the sales deal?" Tiff saw a map of New England in her mind, Maine like a dog's head with ears, Massachusetts like a long-necked dinosaur....

"Providence. But it doesn't matter. What I'm saying is I miss you and—"

"That's not what you used to say," Tiff said. "You told me I was hyper and crazy and you couldn't relax when I was around."

"Yeah, well, sometimes we say things that we wish we hadn't said when we think about them later. I was tired, and I'm sorry."

"That's why you left us." Tiff watched Mom lean against the wall, arms crossed over her chest and one foot tapping. Both of hers were, too.

"No, I was—"

"You told me I was a live wire and a loose cannon and my meds were turning me into a pill-popping junkie. You said you couldn't handle my ups and downs and ins and outs and lefts and rights and...."

Dad turned blurry through her tears and she wiped her eyes. *Damn, she didn't want to cry in front of him.*

"Hey, Princess." Dad put up one hand. "Slow down, OK? That was the past and I'm sorry. But I want to help."

"So much you've missed the last three support payments," Mom said.

"I told you, I'm getting a major raise now. That's not going to be a problem. In fact, that's the other thing I want to toss out here."

"What?"

Dad tipped his glass and brought it away empty.

"Look, this is a lot to take in. Let's slow down, OK?" He looked at Mom and held up the glass. "Can I have another one, Gail?"

"Can you walk all the way to the kitchen?"

"Oh, come on, don't be like that." Dad gave her a little smile and raised his eyebrows. Mom took the glass and didn't quite stomp out the door. When she left, the room felt smaller and Dad felt bigger. Tiff clutched her guitar even more tightly.

"When did you get an electric guitar?" Dad asked.

"About two months ago." Tiff felt like she was giving away a secret. "Some of the guys at school are starting a band and none of them can play lead, so I'm trying to learn...."

"So you're going to try to play with them." Dad's voice sounded so neutral Tiff almost looked at the floor for a trap.

"Well, I'm...."

"A pink guitar."

"I think it's cool." She would never tell him it was the cheapest guitar in the store.

"What do the guys say?"

Mom returned with Dad's fresh beer.

"Sorry I didn't unpack the silver tray and the doilies. They're probably in one of the boxes you're leaning on."

Dad gave her a look.

"Thank you. Um, the other thing I wanted to say, the regional headquarters is in Dedham."

Mom's eyes widened.

"Where's Dedham?" Tiff asked.

"It's near Boston. I'd be moving there."

"And you want her to stay over for weekends." Mom's voice gave Tiff goose bumps.

"You know, there are some really good specialists in Boston. Tiff might get more help than she's getting around here. If she lived with me, she could go to special schools there, maybe get off the meds...."

"Are you out of your mind?" Mom's voice climbed a scale word by word. "You couldn't stand to be with her and now you're saying you want her to live with you. Is that what I'm hearing?"

"What about it, Tiff?" Dad gave her his "sign here" smile. "Your mom said it was up to you. Hey, you like guitar, they've got a great music school in Boston. You ever hear of Berklee?"

Tiff's guitar felt heavy and her posters swirled, the women seeming to scream at her.

"Take your time, don't decide right away." Dad smiled again. "You can think about it for a week."

"Out of the question," Mom said. "I have custody and I won't give it up."

"Good mother." Dad nodded to Tiff's guitar. "Can I try it out?"

"Do you play?" Tiff asked.

"I know a few chords. From when you started lessons, remember?"

Tiff pulled the strap over her head. Dad put his beer glass on the floor by the edge of the mat and took the guitar. He sat in the chair and draped the strap around his neck before he looked back at Mom.

"Good mother," he said again. "I've missed a couple of payments, but I'll bet Tiff's still getting her meds, isn't she?"

Mom's face turned pinker than Tiff's guitar. "What are you saying, Darrell?"

Dad took the strap off and dropped it on the floor behind him. The guitar looked like a ukulele in his lap, and it clashed with his tie.

"Just thinking out loud. You're working overtime for crummy wages but you've bought your daughter a guitar and you're shelling out a hundred and thirty a month for meds. You don't have that money. But you're working at a hospital...."

Mom's eyes flickered around the room. "You're...."

"Now, if I have custody, there's no problem with that, is there? But if you want to fight, I'll make a couple of phone calls and ... well."

Tiff wanted to throw up.

Dad fingered an E chord and strummed. He found the volume knob and turned it up.

"I'm right, aren't I?"

His next chord sounded louder. Mom's throat moved but she didn't say anything.

"Why don't you go in the other room and think about it for a few minutes, Gail? Tiff and I will rock out here while you decide."

"You...." Mom's voice died. She looked at Tiff and then at her ex-husband before she sagged out of the room.

"What are you saying, Daddy?" Tiff felt her voice leap out of her throat. "Are you saying Mom stole the meds? My Ritalin? That's so—"

"Princess, if a nurse is stealing prescription drugs from a hospital, she's a criminal and she'll lose her license. She might even go to jail."

He turned the volume knob up and strummed another chord, a G. Tiff's heart tried to explode through her rib cage.

"And how can she take care of you if she's in jail?"

He turned the volume knob up all the way and slashed across the strings, the chord pounding on her ears.

Slow down, Tiff told herself. *Slow down, slow down, slow down.*

"You can make new friends, Tiff. A new school, other kids who dig music. I'd even bring you down here to visit mom. In jail."

He moved his fingers to a C chord and raised the pick over his head.

His glass of beer stood on the edge of the rug. Tiff kicked it over and watched the pale liquid splash on his tasseled loafers and darken the rug around them. Dad swept his hand down across the strings. For a second, a deep rich chord exploded from the amplifier.

Then the chord turned into a deafening drone, filling the room louder than a million bees. It bounced off the walls, back and forth, back and forth, between the women's faces, Mother Maybelle Carter and Sister Rosetta Tharpe and Taylor Swift and Neko Case, and Tiff put her hands over her ears. Dad's shoulders bent back against the chair but his body arched like that C chord, coming off the seat and pulling him up on his toes. The drone turned into an ear-slicing crackle, drilling into Tiff's head even through her hands until the amp on the metal bookshelf belched smoke and the crackle faded to a buzz, a hum, then silence.

Tiff took her hands from her ears and stared at the women on her walls. She avoided the bathmat and the puddle of beer, forcing herself not to look back at the man with the singed hair, not to reach out and touch him or her guitar. Her feet tapped on the hardwood floor.

The door slammed back against the wall.

"My God, what happened?" Mom took two steps toward her husband, who smelled like scorched pork, before she stopped short of the mat, too. She saw the overturned glass and looked up at Tiff.

"Are you all right?"

Tiff nodded. She wasn't sure she could talk yet.

Mom closed the door behind them and herded her into the living room before she dialed 911. She hung up and pulled Tiff close.

"He's got to have insurance," she whispered. "Pay for his funeral at least."

Her sweatshirt smelled like lemon Pledge. "Maybe a new guitar and amp, too."

Tiff closed her eyes and saw Dad arch back in the chair again. "I was doing my homework, wasn't I?"

Mom pulled back and looked in her eyes. "I was helping you. Damn algebra."

"Yeah."

They looked at the closed door and Mom shook her head.

"That last chord. It sounded like Peter Townshend."

"Who?" Tiff asked.

Mom hugged her again. "Before your time."

They stood there until the siren stopped outside. A few seconds later, someone knocked on the front door.

Steve Liskow (steveliskow.com) has published sixteen novels and dozens of short stories, including crime, romance, supernatural, and the occasional comedy. His stories have appeared in *Alfred Hitchcock's Mystery Magazine, Black Cat Mystery Magazine, Mystery Weekly,* and several anthologies. He has been a finalist for both the Edgar Award and the Shamus Award, and has won the Black Orchid Novella Award twice and Honorable Mention twice more.

BURNIN BUTT, TEXAS
MARK TROY

Ten young women, each wearing identical sequined green blouses and short red skirts, accessorized with red boots, white, wide-cuffed gloves adorned with green sequins, and sequined cowgirl hats, stepped smartly onto the main stage beneath a long banner proclaiming the thirty-ninth annual Burnin Butt, Texas, Jalapeño Fest. "Your Burnin Butt High School Drill Team, the Jalapeño Honeys. Give it up for these lovely ladies," Hank Marlen, the MC, shouted. The Honeys smiled and waved as the festival goers whooped and cheered.

Hank shouted into the mic again. "Now, the stars of the evening, the ten bravest or craziest men and women in Texas. Your Burnin Butt, Butt Burnin' Jalapeño Eatin' Contest participants. Let's hear it for these iron-tongued gladiators."

Another roar as ten people came on stage and took positions behind plastic trays emblazoned with their names arranged on a long table. Marlen introduced them, saving for last the two men who occupied the middle positions.

"Last year's runner-up, Travis 'Fire In The Hole' Walton."

Walton, mid-thirties, brown wavy hair, runner's build, waved to loud cheers.

"And finally, two-time defending champion, Joe 'Mojopeño' Blanco. Let's hear it for the champ." Blanco, shorter and heavier, doffed his Resistol hat to the crowd's adulation.

On a signal from Marlen, each Honey opened a bag of peppers and emptied the contents into the tray of their assigned competitor.

"It's go time, eaters! Get set! Eat!"

Contestants began shoveling dark green bombs of agony into their mouths. At the nine-minute mark, Fire In The Hole and Mojopeño were each on their fourth bag of peppers. At the eleven minute mark, five eaters had dropped out. It was clear that only the two favorites had a chance to win. Blanco and Walton battled it out for the twelfth and last minute.

Hank Marlen began a count down. "Ten ... nine ... eight ..."

The audience joined in. "SEVEN ... SIX ... FIVE ... FOUR ..."

Blanco's cheeks suddenly filled like a chipmunk's. His eyes widened. He covered his mouth with his hand.

"Uh oh, folks. We might have ourselves a Roman reversal."

Blanco's chest heaved. Green mush oozed between his fingers as he fought to keep everything inside. He gave another heave and spewed.

"Looks like Mojopeño's lost his mojo. That makes Fire In The Hole our new champion."

* * * *

When Chief Constable Brian Costello entered the JP's office Monday morning, Justice of the Peace Bob Moreno was watching a TV news update of the contest as a reporter announced that Joe Blanco had died.

"Damn shame," the constable said.

Costello had rushed on stage to Joe Blanco. He had rolled the still-vomiting man onto his side and attempted to clear his airways until the medics arrived. "You think the county can see clear to buying me a new uniform shirt, Judge? I don't think the stink's ever gonna come out."

Moreno snorted.

"Didn't guess so. When's the inquest?"

"Won't be one. Nothing to inquest about."

"No inquest following an unnatural death?"

"Nothing unnatural about dying from eating too many peppers. Eating one hundred eighty-six jalapeños is what's unnatural. Dying is the risk you take."

"That contest has been running for years and nobody died."

"Nobody ever ate one hundred and eighty-six of those damn things, either. Look, if I do an inquest, it'll just stir things up, and things are stirred up enough already. There ain't a dry eye over at the high school today."

Joe Blanco and Trav Walton were both well-known in Burnin Butt. Blanco had grown up on the pepper farms, played tackle when the football team made state. After graduating from A&M, Blanco returned to teach, eventually rising to assistant principal. Walton hailed from Dallas. Came to the Butt five years earlier to teach the AP science classes.

Moreno continued. "Don't need to tell you how important this festival is to the Butt area. The festival board's afraid what might happen if the contest gets a black eye."

Costello's scalp itched as it always did when something seemed corrupt. "So the board wants to put poor ol' Joe Blanco in the ground and expect everybody to forget about it?"

Moreno fixed him narrowly. "Don't go getting all Longmire on me, Constable. Joe Blanco died of heart failure after pushing himself like a champion. He'll be remembered."

Costello replaced his hat. "Died like a champion. Got it."

* * * *

At ten-thirty, Costello found Hank Marlen in Marlen's pit barbecue restaurant. "Mornin' Hank. You got a minute to talk about the festival?"

"Sure thing, Constable. Mighty successful, I say."

"Joe Blanco might disagree."

"Yeah, that was a shock. Who'd guess a man that young would die of heart failure?"

"Technically, they say, everybody dies of heart failure. The only question is what brought it on. I'm wondering did he get hold of a bad pepper. Hoping you could tell me where the peppers came from."

"What do you mean a bad pepper?"

Costello shrugged. "I'm just working back from the last thing he was doing before he died, which was eating peppers."

"Constable, the whole idea behind the festival is that eating peppers are good for you. You go around saying the peppers are dangerous, nobody'll come."

"Didn't say they're dangerous, Hank."

Marlen waved away Costello's objection. "People all know I was responsible for getting the peppers. If folks're saying those peppers was bad, I'll be out of business faster than I can inject a brisket."

"So help me eliminate the peppers as a problem."

Marlen had Costello follow him into the kitchen. He opened a walk-in cooler and wheeled out a two-tiered serving cart. The lower tier held peppers in plastic bags. The upper tier was stacked with plastic food storage containers, each bearing the name of a contestant.

Marlen lifted a bag from the lower tier. "The leftovers. If there was a problem, like poison or something, it oughta show up here. We keep these for awhile in case of a challenge to the results. I'll be glad to have the cooler space back."

"People challenge the results?" Costello asked

"For a five thousand dollar top prize, somebody might. Don't expect so this time, though. Walton's the clear winner. Mighta been a challenge from Blanco or the other way around if Blanco had survived. Sorry, bad choice of words. If Blanco hadn't been disqualified. Only a pepper or two between them. The next person was at least fifteen behind."

Marlen explained that before the contest they'd filled the bags with fifty peppers each. The bags were then loaded into a bin on stage. The Honeys drew from the bin. "So the peppers a contestant gets are simply luck of the draw."

Costello indicated the storage boxes. "What's in these?"

Marlen lifted the top one with Walton's name. The lid was sealed, but the contents were visible. Costello saw four empty bags and some intact jalapeños surrounded by green pepper caps and stems.

Costello counted fifteen uneaten peppers. "Four bags, so two hundred minus fifteen. Walton ate one hundred eighty-five."

"Officially, one eighty-four. We discounted one pepper because too much of the cap remained."

"Blanco ate one eighty-six. He'd have won."

"Can't say for sure," Marlen said. "We didn't do an official count of the caps. What would be the point? The reversal disqualified him."

Costello was thinking that if anyone had a motive to kill Blanco, it was Walton, but he didn't see how, given the random way the peppers were bagged and distributed. "Let me have Blanco's container." When Marlen hesitated, he said, "The man's dead. He won't challenge."

Marlen handed it over and Costello carried it out of the restaurant. He climbed into his truck and headed out of town. An hour later, he arrived at a Whataburger on Highway 59 in Laredo. Inside, near the head of the order line was a familiar figure that made his pulse quicken. He moved up behind her and put his arm around her waist.

"Thanks for saving me a spot, Kacey."

"The hell, Brian. Do you know how long I waited? I'm supposed to be back at the lab in twenty-five. You're buying."

Costello had called Kacey Schulman after leaving Burnin Butt and arranged to meet at this Whataburger a few miles from the DPS crime lab where Kacey was a technician. There was another Whataburger closer to DPS, but Brian didn't want to risk being seen by other techs or by Kacey's husband.

He had met Kacey at a law enforcement workshop three years before. They felt an instant attraction which soon turned physical. However, the relationship lasted only as long as the workshop. There had been a few meetings in the interim, but although the attraction remained, they'd mutually agreed that to continue the affair would be dangerous.

They took their meals out to Costello's truck and sat on the tailgate with the burgers, fries, and drinks between them. Costello told her about the contest and Joe Blanco's death.

"You really think somebody poisoned him?" Kacey asked.

"He ate and he died. Hoping you can tell me why."

"What did the inquest say?"

"No inquest. The town fathers are afraid an inquest will kill the cash cow."

"So you're going off the books."

"Something like that."

"And you want me to help you? Also off the books?"

"I get that it's a lot to ask."

"For just a Whataburger?"

"Something happened that ain't right. Joe Blanco needs to be answered for."

"I don't know, Brian."

"I'll throw in a shake and supersize the fries next time. Look, Kacey, I really need help on this, and you're the one with the smarts to do it."

"Last time I heard that, you were trying to get into my pants."

"I might still if I thought there was a chance."

"So long as you understand that chance is gone, what've you got?"

Costello retrieved the food container and brought it back to the gate. He opened the lid and explained how the peppers were packaged.

Kacey took a pen from her purse and began pushing the caps into piles. "He ate all these?"

"Yep."

Soon she had nine piles of pepper caps, twenty in each pile. Nine caps remained.

"How many did you say he ate?"

"Hundred eighty-six."

"I count a hundred eighty-nine."

"You counted wrong, Kacey. Fourteen peppers are left in the bag."

"You count."

Costello counted the caps. "One eighty-nine. But there were only four bags. Fifty in each."

"Somehow he got three extra. You have a problem, Brian."

"Somebody wanted him to eat three extra peppers. You think what I'm thinking?"

"Your murder weapons."

Costello's phone rang. He checked the screen. "Shit. Rob Moreno. He probably talked to Hank Marlen."

"Are you in trouble?"

"Probably about to be fired, but he'll have to do it to my face."

"Seriously? Fired?"

"Unless I can come back with something. Even then, it's not a given."

"Holy cheeseburger, Brian. Now I'm saving your ass for that Whataburger?"

"You're an angel. Could you tell what the poison is?"

"There might be some traces on the three caps, but which ones are they?"

"Wait. I have something else." Costello went into his truck and returned with a plastic bag. When he opened it, a foul odor of garlic and rotten fish arose.

"Eww." Kacey pinched her nose. "What is that?"

"Blanco threw up on my shirt. There might be traces of the poison in it."

"You had to bring this out at lunch?"

* * * *

Costello called the TV station manager to ask about the footage from the contest. He learned that the station had bought the footage from Justin Spahn, the senior editor of the high school newspaper. He drove to the school and checked in at the office where he was given directions to a room in a temporary building. There he found Justin hunched over a keyboard at one of two workstations. Besides the computers, the room contained a printer, supply cabinet, bookcase, and worktable piled with printouts and back issues of the paper.

Costello introduced himself. "You're the one recorded the eating contest, right?"

"Is this about Mr. Blanco's death?"

"It could be."

"Was he murdered?"

"Why do you ask that?"

"You're a police officer, aren't you?"

"Constable."

"Whatever. I don't think you came asking about the video without suspicions."

"Show me." Costello pulled up a chair.

"This could be the biggest story to break in Burnin Butt. If I show you, I want to be the one writes the story."

"I'll update you on anything that turns up."

Justin brought up the video on the monitor. His camera was steady as first the Honeys and then the contestants took the stage. Watching the contestants greet each other, Costello saw something wrong. Blanco and Walton did not shake hands. Instead, they exchanged hostile looks. Costello had Justin replay it.

"For colleagues, they don't look none to friendly."

Justin's expression had gone serious. "I ... I ... might have started something."

"Started what?"

Justin engaged the other monitor. He opened a file and a list of names appeared. "The most recent senior honor roll. It hasn't been made public yet. What do you see?"

Costello studied the list, a total of ten names. "Mostly female. Two males. You know them?"

Justin nodded. "Four of the girls are on the drill team."

"So?"

"They're sorta hot, but not the sharpest knives."

"Maybe they applied themselves real hard this semester."

"Yeah, and there's good Mexican food north of I-20. This is their last year. Each of them is taking a light load in terms of hours, but the courses are supposed to be hard. They're AP courses taught by Mr. Walton."

"What are you getting at?"

"So I interviewed some of the guys in the class. They're grumbling that they don't receive a fair shake and the girls get the top grades."

"What about these two males on the list?"

"They're not in his classes. Both dropped and are taking online. Some of the other guys are thinking about doing that."

"So how does this relate to Blanco?"

"I told Mr. Blanco about the disparity. Gave him transcripts of interviews. He said he would read what I wrote and we'd talk about it. We were set to meet today. Mr. Blanco might have talked to Mr. Walton. Could that bear on what happened?"

Costello wasn't ready to come to a conclusion. "Run it again from the start."

This time, he focused on the line of lithe young women marching in precision onto the stage. Justin identified each one as they came across. "Meredith Bauer and Cathy Carter. They're both on the honor list. Hayley Davis, she's the captain."

As Hayley, a pretty blonde, crossed center stage, there was a momentary break in the order. Hayley stopped and the girl behind her, a long-legged brunette, nearly ran into her. Hayley made a slight head bob and the other girl resumed stride and marched past her. "Carmela Marlen. She's first lieutenant. They must have lined up wrong. Told you they're not the smartest girls."

When all the Honeys were in place, Hayley stood behind Blanco and Carmela behind Walton.

The video continued. Now Costello focused his attention on Blanco and Walton. How had Blanco ended up with three more peppers than Walton? The bad blood between them made Walton the obvious suspect. But aside from the initial exchange, the two men ignored each other, concentrating on consuming jalapeños.

The end of the contest came and Costello, to his disappointment, had seen no stray peppers make their way to Blanco's tray. While Blanco heaved on screen, Costello tried to gauge Walton's reaction. His face registered first surprise, followed by concern and anxiety. Walton didn't expect that, he thought. The other contestants showed similar reactions. Any murderer among them was a damn good actor.

* * * *

The next morning, Costello went to the school early and waited in the parking lot for Walton's arrival. Walton parked in a reserved slot between two other vehicles. Costello approached Walton's truck from behind, moving into the space between the bed and the neighboring sedan as Walton exited. With his door still open and Costello filling the space behind him, Walton had nowhere to go.

"Congratulations on winning the contest, champ. Quite an accomplishment."

Walton faced him. "It doesn't feel like much of an accomplishment, considering the way it ended."

"Is your asshole still on fire? One hundred eighty-four peppers, right?"

"Vanilla ice cream's doing the trick. What can I do for you, Constable?"

Costello stepped into Walton's space. He had put on his Luccheses with the two-inch heels, which gave him a height advantage over Walton. "I'm just trying to plumb the depths of y'all's rivalry, you could say."

Walton tried to back up, but the open door blocked his escape. "I wouldn't say there's any depth to our rivalry. It was all in fun."

"Y'all didn't shake hands Saturday on stage. If it's a fun rivalry, how come?"

"You might be mistaken, Constable. I think we did."

"Not on the video, Mr. Walton. You shook with everybody but Joe Blanco."

"In the excitement of the contest I don't remember. You know, I think we shook before coming up on stage."

Costello removed his hat and scratched his itching scalp. "So you remember shaking off stage, but you don't remember if y'all did or didn't on stage. Is that correct?"

Walton looked at him suspiciously. "Why are you asking? What difference does it make?"

"Just curious." Costello replaced his hat. "Like you say, it's easy to forget in the excitement of the contest."

"If we're done, Constable, I have work to do."

Costello stood his ground. "There is something else, champ. My niece is a student here. Her mom, my sister, is a single mom, working two jobs, so I'm kinda helping out with my niece's education."

"Very admirable, Constable. I don't believe I've met your niece."

"Wouldn't think so. She's just a freshman, but she's set on being a Jalapeño Honey. You familiar with those girls?"

"A little. I have some in my classes."

"Terrific. My niece is very bright." Costello made a gesture of humility with his hands. "Gets it from her mother."

"That, I can believe, Constable."

"Yeah, well she wants to take some AP courses. Did I say she's bright? Anyway, she asks around and hears from some of these Honeys that they recommend your courses."

"I'm always glad to hear students appreciate my courses, Constable."

"So they tell her that girls do better in your courses than the boys."

Walton shrugged. "If they do, it's because girls at this age are better focused, more mature. Boys are still struggling with hormones."

"It's all about maturity and hormones?"

"I'm not a psychologist, Constable. A guidance counselor could answer that."

"Hate for her to skate through a course because she's a girl."

"Not in my courses, she won't."

"Or because she's a Jalapeño Honey." Costello backed up two steps to permit Walton to close his door.

Walton said, "Been real, Constable." He turned and headed to the school.

"So there was nothing between you and Joe Blanco?" Costello called after him.

Walton didn't reply.

* * * *

Costello's mind ranged over the possibilities of something going on between Walton and his female students. Travis Walton wouldn't be the first male teacher whose head was turned by a sweet smile and a short skirt. If all that came of it was a few extra points on a homework assignment, he deserved a reprimand. Nor would he be the first to fall for the blandishments of a sexy student intent on seducing him. That would bring scandal and loss of employment, at least. The third possibility was that he was using his position of authority to prey on young women, which would mean prison. Of the three, avoiding prison was a motive for murder. But which possibility was it and what did Blanco know?

The other two legs of the murder stool were shakier. Opportunity? Plenty, but nowhere on the video did Walton appear to take it. Means? That was in Kacey's hands.

Kacey called in the afternoon. "You fired yet?"

"Been avoiding him for a full day. Can't avoid him much longer."

"I might have a lifeline for you. Your killer has a Llano pocket gopher problem. That garlicy odor in the vomit on your shirt? Phosphine."

"What's phosphine?"

"The product of a reaction between zinc phosphide and stomach acid. I won't go into the details of how it works, but it's bad news for gophers."

"And humans?"

"If the dose is large enough. Usually, a farmer fails to take the proper precaution in handling, doesn't wear gloves, for example. Somehow they transfer the poison from their hand to their food which makes them sick, and that's it. A death is going to take more than incidental contact. This was a large dose."

"How did he get it? On the peppers?"

"No residue on the intact peppers, but I didn't expect any. If the peppers were dipped in poison, the amount needed to kill would have sickened anybody who handled them. Also, there was no poison in the plastic bags they came from."

"Then where?'

"It must have been inside the peppers. You've got a membrane and seeds inside, but also a lot of space. You need a way to inject it, but you might push five or six milliliters into a fat one. Fifteen milliliters might be enough to kill."

Brian's excitement picked up. What had Hank Marlen said? "Faster than I can inject a brisket."

Kacey continued. "Another thing, zinc phosphide is not easy to get. You need a permit and an infestation, not just one little rodent."

"So, if I had a list of who has a permit—"

"Done and done, Brian. Check your inbox. You're welcome."

"Thanks, Kacey. I owe you a Whataburger."

"Double fries and a shake," she reminded him,

Costello thought about what he'd learned. If Marlen had access to zinc phosphide, that gave him means and opportunity. Hank had procured all the jalapeños. He could have easily injected the poison and inserted the poisoned peppers into the contest bags.

But why add three extra peppers instead of replacing three? Adding peppers increased the risk of discovery. More importantly, if Joe Blanco was Marlen's target, how could he be sure Blanco got the bad peppers? And what was his motive? Nothing so far had pointed to bad blood between the two men. Had he, perhaps, planned to kill indiscriminately? Costello dismissed that notion. Marlen profited from the success of the festival. He was on the board. No way would he do something that would taint the event.

Costello found Kacey's email and clicked the attachment. A short list of farms authorized to use zinc phosphide opened up. Marlen was not among them.

His phone rang. Kacey Schulman again. "I forgot to ask, did your vic wear a costume?"

"Costume? Like what?" Costello thought back to the contest. All contestants wore T-shirts. Blanco's, he remembered, had his nickname, MOJOPEÑO, across his chest.

"I'm thinking dance costume, Brian. I found a green sequin stuck to one of the pepper caps. Looked like it had gotten snagged by the stem. It's colored like a pepper, so it was easy to miss."

"Son of a bitch," Costello said.

* * * *

At three-thirty, Brian Costello drove up Davis Lane, which wound through acres of Davis Farms pepper plants. Sonya Rios, his part-time reserve deputy, followed in a cruiser. Brian had called Justin, who asked around and learned that the senior drill team officers met at Hayley Davis's pool every Tuesday.

Costello and Rios followed a path around the Davis home to the rear from which they heard female voices. Four girls were drinking margaritas at one end of the pool. Wearing swimsuits, their hair wet and faces devoid of makeup, they looked younger than they had on stage. Costello put names to faces. Hayley Davis, Carmela Marlen, Meredith Bauer, and Cathy Carter.

The girls fell silent when Costello and Rios entered the pool deck. Rios said, "Ladies, please leave the pool."

Hayley Davis pushed away from the side of the pool. "This is my home. We don't have to if we don't want to."

Costello said, "It would be better for y'all to do what the officer asks."

Hayley returned a defiant stare and said nothing. Cathy Carter, whom Costello noticed had reacted with open mouth and wide eyes to their presence, said, "I'm going to be sick." She climbed out of the pool and threw up in the grass.

Rios gave the order again. Carmela Marlen said, "We don't have a choice." She got out.

Meredith Bauer turned to Hayley. "I told you this would happen."

"Shut up, Meredith." Hayley gave Meredith a shove, which caused her to lose balance and go under water. Hayley started after her, but Rios jumped into the water and pulled them apart. Rios grabbed Hayley by the arm and dragged her to the steps. Hayley tried to resist, but she was no match for Rios.

Costello picked up some towels from a chaise and tossed them to the girls. He offered one to Rios who declined. He turned to the girls. "Y'all sit, ladies."

Meredith and Carmela took seats on one chaise. Cathy squeezed in beside Carmela, leaving Hayley to take a lone seat on another chaise.

Rios looked at Meredith, "Do you have something to tell us?"

Meredith shook her head.

Cathy began crying. "We're—We're sorry."

"About what?" Costello asked.

"You shut your cock holster," Hayley said.

"About Mr. Blanco," Cathy said.

Costello looked from one to the other. "Tell us what happened, ladies."

Hayley crossed her arms in defiance. "He got sick on stage. What else is there?"

Costello said, "Someone injected poison into the peppers he ate." He turned to Carmela. "I contacted your father. He's missing a meat injector from his restaurant. Any idea where it is?"

"No."

Costello noted that her gaze strayed toward a counter and sink in an outdoor kitchen area. He went over to it. The sink was empty, but beneath it was a panel, which slid out to reveal a kitchen garbage can. He lifted the lid and looked in. Then he carried the can back to Carmela, who broke down in tears.

Hayley yelled, "Leave that alone. That's private property." She sprang from the chaise and ran at Costello.

Rios caught Hayley, who turned to beat on the officer's chest. Rios managed to constrain her. She forced the girl back down. The other Honeys remained in their seats.

Costello said, "Constable Rios, look in the can and tell me what you see."

Rios bent over the can. "I see a meat injector and five peppers. They're split open and they have something inside them."

"Don't touch. I suspect that something is gopher poison, which is used here on this farm. We'll have a lab confirm. I'm guessing these peppers are y'all's first attempts, is that right, ladies? Some trial and error to get the amount right without splitting the peppers?"

All the girls except Hayley sat with downcast eyes. Hayley stared straight ahead. Costello focused on her. "We know how it went down. You had three of them inside the cuff of your glove and you dropped them into Mr. Blanco's tray when you emptied the first bag of peppers."

Hayley sneered. "Try to prove that."

"It's on video. I missed it at first, because the peppers are the exact color of your uniform, but we were able to enhance the video enough to see them drop. When we get your glove, we'll find it missing a sequin, which ended up on one of the peppers."

"But why?" Rios asked.

Meredith raised her head. "He wouldn't stop. He kept insisting on more."

"More what?" Rios asked.

"Sex," Meredith and Cathy answered together.

Cathy said, "It started off as just wine and pot parties. Then it was kissing. And then—"

"I lollipopped him because he insisted," Meredith said.

Carmela nodded. "We had sex in his office when we were supposed to be discussing grades."

"In the assistant principal's office?" Costello asked.

"No, not Mr. Blanco. He was a good man. He wasn't supposed to die. It was supposed to be Mr. Walton, but she changed it." Carmela aimed a finger at Hayley. "You switched places. I thought you were calling it off."

Hayley's eyes flashed in anger. "Call it off and let that animal get away with what he did to us?"

"He needed to be punished," Meredith said.

"He is being punished. Now he knows we own him. Don't you see? We saved his job and at the same time implicated him. He's ours to command."

"He was supposed to die," Cathy said.

"And if he did, what would happen to me?"

"Explain yourself," Costello said.

Rios had been looking in the garbage can. She turned it over and spilled its contents on the floor. "Here's the answer." Mixed with the peppers was a home pregnancy test.

Costello asked, "Is one of you pregnant?"

Hayley said, "I couldn't let him die. I couldn't let him leave. I need to keep him with me. Now he owes me and the baby."

"Won't be happening," Costello said.

Carmela glared at Hayley. "All because you lost a sequin."

"Demerit for not taking care of your costume," Rios said.

Costello said, "Hayley Davis, stand up. Y'all are under arrest for the murder of Joe Blanco. As are the rest of you ladies."

Hayley stood, but instead of turning around, she lunged at the peppers on the floor and scooped up three of them. Before Costello cold stop her, she shoved them into her mouth, bit into them, and swallowed.

* * * *

Costello met Kacey Schulman at the Highway 59 Whataburger.

Kacey said, "That's some twisted town you got up there in Burnin Butt, Brian. You think the Jalapeño Honeys will be back kickin' again anytime soon?"

"Not at football games," he said. "Right now, they're kicking each other, pointing fingers and trying to cut deals. They're aiming most of their kicks at Haley Davis."

"Is she gonna live?"

"Appears so. Rios was the hero. She got her finger down Haley's throat and forced her to vomit."

Kacey screwed up her face in disgust. "If you brought me another shirt, I'll kill you, Brian."

"Just Whataburger this time." He placed a bag between them on the tailgate.

"What about the creepy teacher?"

"His teaching career's done. Lookin' at possible sexual assault charges that he's tryin' to plea down. The shame, as I see it, is they can't get him for any part of the murder, because he didn't know about it."

"Yet all of this comes back to him."

"Yep. About as messed up as pig shit on a hoe handle."

"So, you fired or not?" Kacey asked.

"Not, though I'm not for sure I want to continue working for a JP who answers to the festival board."

"Hear that," Kacey said. She opened the Whataburger bag Costello had placed on the tailgate. "Double fries and a shake. Some things aren't messed up."

"Y'all know they're not Texan anymore, doncha? Some Yankees in Chicago own 'em all now."

Kacey sighed. "You're really some piece of work, you know that, Brian? I save your ass and you pay me with a counterfeit burger."

Mark Troy is the author of the Shamus nominated *Pilikia Is My Business* and the Claymore Dagger finalist *The Splintered Paddle*. His short story, "Shaft on Wheels," appeared in *The Eyes of Texas: Private Eyes from the Panhandle to the Piney Woods*, an anthology edited by Michael Bracken. Mark's novella *Dos Tacos Guatemaltecos y Una Pistola Casera* was episode twelve, season two of the *Guns + Tacos* series. Mark lives in College Station, Texas. When not writing, he mixes knock-you-on-your-ass tiki cocktails.

THE AFFAIR OF LAMSON'S COOK

CHARLES FELTON PIDGIN & J.M. TAYLOR

(Originally appeared in *The Chronicles of Quincy Adams Sawyer, Detective* (1912))

Quincy sauntered slowly along the street, enjoying the sunny warmth of an early June morning. Few cases had been presented to him of late, and the resulting inactivity had served to stock him, both mentally and physically, with unusual energy. His keen eyes, restless with inaction, flashed hither and thither over the small throng of hurrying pedestrians, as though in search of something on which to exercise his peculiar talents. But the people surrounding him seemed productive of anything other than mysteries. They comprised mainly the usual throng of hurrying clerks, stenographers and other employees, all rushing toward their individual desks or stations, and whatever secrets might be buried in their minds were for the present, at least, successfully forgotten or covered. With a deep sigh at the possibility of another day of quiet and solitude, Quincy turned slowly in the direction of his own office, but paused sharply as the sound of a call reached his ears.

"Sawyer! Oh, I say, Sawyer!" came the half-suppressed shout, and Quincy's eyes, flashing sharply over the street, instantly picked out the source of the call.

Slowly bearing down on him, through the press of market wagons, trucks and other early morning vehicles, came a handsome touring car. At the wheel sat an impassive French chauffeur and in the tonneau a fat, puffy little man danced frantically about for all the world like a huge bullfrog in a net. Quincy recognized the man as Herbert Lamson, prominent clubman, first-nighter, and society leader in general, and wondered vaguely what unseemly occurrence could have brought Lamson out at that early hour of the morning. He halted and stood smiling interrogatively as the machine drew up at the curb.

"Oh, I say, Sawyer!" Lamson puffed, as soon as the car had been brought to a halt. "It's a lucky I found you, you know. I want you to come right out to my house without a moment's delay. We've had a frightful occurrence there. Frightful!"

"Which house?" Quincy inquired, ignoring the door which Lamson held invitingly open.

"My country house, Sawyer. The one at Beverly. Come right away, won't you? It's an awful thing and I simply must have help!"

"But what is it? What has happened?" Quincy questioned, not relishing the idea of being dragged down to Beverly to discover who had thrown a pebble through one of Lamson's plate glass windows, which possibility, knowing Lamson as well as he did, Quincy deemed not improbable.

"It's murder, Sawyer, murder!" Lamson spluttered, spitting out the word as though it choked him and gazing helplessly at Quincy through his round, sheep-like eyes. "Somebody brutally murdered my cook last night—and she could cook the best fish dinners I ever tasted."

Quincy barely repressed a desire to laugh at the incongruity of the two statements, knowing well that the only method of endearing oneself to Lamson was through the medium of the latter's digestive system. For a moment only he hesitated, then, swinging into the car beside Lamson, he settled back for the ride to Beverly.

"Now, Lamson," he said, when the car had drawn away from the mid-city tumult, "give me some of the details of this case, so that I may be prepared to act when we arrive. Just when, so far as you can tell, did the murder take place?"

"I can't say just when," Lamson informed him. "I was away from the house from five o'clock in the afternoon until late last night. It might have been done while I was away, or after I returned, because she was not discovered until early this morning. One of the maids, according to custom, went to call her in time to prepare breakfast, and found her dead. I was immediately notified and, not knowing what else to do, I hurried up after you. I'll catch that murderer, Sawyer, if it costs me my entire fortune," he broke off savagely. "That woman was a downright shrew, but she could cook—Lord bless you! she could cook! And now I must spend a year or two hunting another cook, and I shall probably be obliged to live on all manner of horrible dishes during my search. I know I can never find another who will be able to cook fish the way she could!" He seemed saddened, almost to the point of breaking down, at the last thought.

"I understand, Lamson," said Quincy, after a protracted coughing fit behind his hand. "But I want to get the facts of the case itself, the murder. How was she murdered, and do you suspect anybody? Now, give me something of that sort to work on. First, what was her name, where did she come from, and how long had she been with you?"

"Her name," said Lamson in a saddened voice, apparently engendered by the thought of the fish dinners which were to be his no more, "was Mrs. Elizabeth Buck. She had been with me as cook for about twelve years, but I have no idea where she came from originally. You see, I was obliged to hire her rather hastily at a time when I was giving a dinner and my other cook—"

"Yes, yes," Quincy hurriedly interrupted, "but had she any relatives or friends who wrote to her, or with whom she visited?"

"Nobody of whom I ever heard. In fact, from the time when I first engaged her, I do not believe she has been away from my house a single day. Her sharp temper would rather preclude the possibility of her having any friends, and I doubt if there was a person in the world, outside myself, in whom she felt the slightest interest."

"Now," said Quincy approvingly, "you are started right. Give me all the details you can up to the time when the body was discovered."

"Well, she was a woman who, as I said, apparently had neither friends nor acquaintances. Therefore, I do not think that the affair occurred because of some old grudge a previous associate may have owed her. Since I have been talking with you a possibility, which hitherto had not occurred to me, has come into my mind. I paid her well, very well, and, as I never knew of her spending much money at a time, she must have been able to lay by quite a bit in the last twelve years. Of course she may have kept her money in a savings bank, but it is equally possible that her distrustful nature led her to hide it somewhere about her house. She did not room in my house, but in a little cottage which stood on the grounds, living by herself. Now the possibility I mentioned, and which, at the time when left, had not been investigated, is that somebody may have murdered her for her money. Damn 'em! I'd have given them an equal amount gladly, if they'd only have let her live to cook for me.

"In person she was a small woman of perhaps fifty, although she was so wizened and dried-up by nature that she might have been either more or less. In fact, her appearance has never changed since I have known her. She was very small in stature, and, although I think she would have been capable of putting up a stiff fight, she would have been no match, of course, for an ordinarily strong man. Last night, the servants say, she retired to her cottage at her usual time, and nothing was heard of her during the evening. Very early this morning one of the maids went to call her and, receiving no response to her knock, pushed open the door and found the body.

"The woman had been stabbed, and the place was in a terrible state of disorder; but that part of it you can see for yourself when we get there. I left orders that nobody should enter the building, and that nothing was to be disturbed until I returned. On making the discovery, the maid rushed from the house screaming, and fell on the lawn in a dead faint. I was at once called, and by the time the maid had regained her senses, I was on the spot. As soon as she had told her story I looked hastily into the woman's house to verify the facts, and hurried to Boston to secure your services. You are, of course, to do whatever you think best in the matter, and I give you full authority to act in any way you may deem necessary on my premises."

For a few moments, following the recital, Quincy was silent, knowing well that little further information was to be gained until he should arrive at the grounds and be able to examine the premises in person.

"How did you come to employ the woman when you had absolutely no knowledge of her, or of her previous state of life?" he asked, after a time.

"Why, I told you that I was obliged to have a cook in great haste at that time," Lamson protested. "She was well recommended as a cook by the employment agency and consequently I hired her with very little question. I have never had any trouble whatever with her and in the twelve years I had come to look on her as being scrupulously honest and trustworthy in every way. But wait, we are nearly there now, and you will soon have an opportunity to judge this matter at first hand."

Quincy stared unseeingly at the low and dirty wooden buildings which lined the street along which the machine was speeding. The case appealed strongly to him as it had been rehearsed, and he could not suppress a certain intangible feeling that it would grow yet more interesting as it progressed. Of course, he considered, in case of a murder for the purpose of robbery, at the possibility of which Lamson hinted, the case would undoubtedly degenerate into a mere police routine affair in which he could take no part. But, on the other hand, the very air of mystery which appeared to surround the woman, herself, gave a vague promise of possibilities into which he would be able to dig and search to his heart's content. He glanced once more at his surroundings, and discovered that they were now in more open country and that the dirty little buildings had given place to the more imposing residences of Beverly's summer colony. The machine turned abruptly, and he discovered that they were rolling up a curved driveway to what was undoubtedly Lamson's house.

A much agitated servant hurried up to the machine as they alighted and, after a somewhat doubtful glance at Quincy, reported in a rapid undertone:

"The police are here, sir, and the medical examiner. I told them of my orders against allowing anybody to enter the cook's house until you had returned with a detective, and they consented to wait. They are down under the tree by the house now."

"All right, Higgins," Lamson replied, turning once more toward Quincy. "Now, Mr. Sawyer, if you will come right down we can all examine the rooms together. I am somewhat surprised that the police consented to await my return. They are usually little inclined to await the convenience of a private detective, are they not?"

"Unfortunately, they are," Quincy replied with a dry smile. "The police in a large city would not have done so, under any circumstances; but it is probable that in these smaller towns the police and all other municipal officials are more ready to pay heed to the wishes of their wealthy residents. It is out of respect to you, and through no regard for me, that they are waiting."

Quincy carefully examined the exterior of the cook's former place of residence as they approached. It was a pretty little cottage, painted a conservative white and standing in a location considerably removed from the residence of Lamson himself. The cottage was of fair dimensions, containing, he judged, about six rooms; but it appeared dwarfed because of the giant horse-chestnut trees which towered above it on every side. From beneath one of these trees three men arose and came forward to meet them, Quincy having an excellent opportunity to examine the officials as they advanced.

The foremost of the trio he judged, by reason of the bountiful supply of gold braid sprinkled over his uniform, to be the chief of the local department. The second, who followed at a respectful distance, was evidently a member of the force, while the last, a rather small, dark-faced man in plain clothes, was undoubtedly the medical examiner. As Quincy and Lamson halted before the house, the chief bustled up to them, a smile, which was evidently intended to be courteous, playing across his ordinarily pompous features.

"We have been waiting some time for you, Mr. Lamson," he remarked; "but under the circumstances we were willing to delay our work until your return. The affair undoubtedly will prove a simple one, and it is too bad you have gone to the expense of importing a private detective." With the concluding words he shot a brief, but unfriendly, glance in Quincy's direction.

Lamson made no reply to the speech, other than by a brief nod of recognition, and, stepping quickly to the door, he unlocked it and threw it open, standing aside to allow the entrance of the officials. Like a pack of hounds unleashed the local men dived through the door, and into what was apparently a living room, Quincy and Lamson following in their rear. On entering the room all paused abruptly and stared about them, the scene well warranting the sudden halt.

The room was, indeed, in a terrible state of disorder. Furniture had been overturned, some had been broken, all had been misplaced, and on every hand were to be seen signs of violence and confusion. The main feature, however, was to be found in the figure of a little woman who lay almost in the very middle of the room. The body lay face down, the hair disheveled and the clothing disarranged from the struggle, while from its side and several inches below the left armpit protruded the hilt of a heavy and strong-bladed knife. There were very few signs of blood, as the wound had evidently bled inwardly; but the scene was ghastly enough without that.

Exercising the prerogative of his office, the medical examiner strode forward and knelt at the side of the body, gently turning it over. As he did so the watchers instinctively started, for on the woman's face was revealed such an expression of fierce and malignant hatred as it is seldom the misfortune of any person to gaze on. The lips were drawn back in a snarl of rage which left exposed the worn and ragged teeth, and the eyes, fixed and staring, seemed to hold in their depths a fury scarcely human.

"Lord!" muttered Lamson, repressing a shudder. "She didn't die with any love of man in her heart."

The medical examiner grimly held up the knife. "From here on it's your work, gentlemen," he observed. "Make what you can of this."

The chief took the knife, and all stared curiously at it. It was an ordinary wooden-hilted knife of the kind to be found in any market and, from the thinness of the blade, it had evidently known long service and many grindings. After nodding his head over it several times, the chief passed the knife on to Quincy with the air of a man wishing to be courteous, although hardly recognizing the possibility of any value in the act. To Quincy, judging from his expression, the knife meant much or nothing. He glanced at it keenly, turned it over several times and then, without comment, returned it to the chief.

The search for clues then started in earnest, the two members of the regular force burrowing amidst the debris in the room like terriers after a rat. They pulled open every drawer, peered under or through every article of furniture, and minutely examined every square inch of space in the room. Now and then the chief would pause to glance speculatively at Quincy, as though in fear that the private detective might stumble on a clue that the regulars had overlooked. After each scrutiny, however, he invariably returned to his search, appeared satisfied that Quincy's aimless wanderings would net him nothing of value in the way of clues.

"By the way, Chief," Quincy interrupted at length, "may I inquire as to what it is that you expect to find in this room?"

The chief eyed him suspiciously before replying. "Well, it's not customary to hand our suspicions to outsiders, but, as you are, in a way, one of us, I don't mind telling you. Of course we are looking for possible clues which the murderer may have left behind, but primarily I want to discover whether or not the old woman's hoard of money is missing."

"I see, Chief; but, unless we know, which we do not, where the money was hidden, how are we to be able to tell whether or not it is gone? We suspect, of course, but we do not know, that there was money hidden in the house. It is hardly likely that the woman would have kept any quantity of it hidden away in a bureau drawer. It strikes me that if she had money to hide she would have placed it in a more secret hiding-place—under the floor boards, behind a stone in the cellar wall, or in some similar crevice. We might search a week and still not find the place. And, even if we should chance to find the money, all we should have gained would be a knowledge that the murderer did not take it. Look over the room. There was no search for money previous to our coming. That furniture was all disarranged during the struggle. Either the murderer knew exactly where the money was hidden, and took it from its hiding-place, or else he was actuated by some other motive entirely and had neither thought nor regard for the money that might be here."

The chief listened stolidly to Quincy's summing up of the matter; but he seemed unimpressed. "You are at liberty to follow any method you please in the conduct of your search," he said coldly; "but the regular police must act under my orders, and I see no necessity for changing the orders because of your ingenious theory. I am experienced in these matters, Mr. Sawyer, and I judge that you are not; so please don't confuse my men by advancing any other theories. This murder was for the purpose of robbery, and for no other purpose under the sun."

Quincy meekly accepted the rebuff without reply, but there was a peculiar smile playing about his lips as he turned away. Apparently undisturbed, he wandered nonchalantly out of the room, with Lamson, angered at the treatment his special representative had received, trailing behind. To the remaining rooms on the first floor Quincy paid only the most casual notice, doing little more than to glance in each before ascending the stairs. On the second floor, however, his interest appeared to awaken, especially when the woman's chamber had been reached.

Once within the chamber his aimless wandering ceased, and his every movement appeared to take on a definite purpose. He glanced sharply over the walls, carefully scrutinizing the few pictures with which they were adorned, after which he stepped briskly to the bureau, where he conducted a most minute examination of the contents of every drawer. Once he paused and held up a small packet before the gaze of Lamson, grinning as he did so.

"I imagine our friends downstairs would be interested in this," he remarked.

"What are they?" Lamson questioned eagerly.

"Bank books. Your late cook evidently patronized several savings banks, instead of hoarding her money as has been suspected. I'll place them back where they were, and let the police discover them when they reach this point in their search. At their present rate of speed they should reach this room in a day or two."

For some little time, after the discovery of the books, he remained before the bureau, searching every nook and cranny of it. At last, appearing vastly dissatisfied with the result, he arose and stood meditatively in the middle of the room, allowing his eyes to run rapidly over first one article of furniture and then another.

"Did your cook have a trunk when she came here?" he questioned abruptly.

"I don't think so," said Lamson slowly, as he strived to remember the event of twelve years previous. "No, I am sure she brought with her one of those old-fashioned canvas extension bags. It must be around here somewhere."

Quincy's interest appeared to renew itself at the information, and he was immediately deep in his search again. At last, with much shuffling and scuffling of his feet, he emerged backward from a dark nook in the closet, dragging after him the described bag. Placing it on the floor, he arose and stared at Lamson through eyes shining with eagerness.

"Lamson," he said, "I expect to find the clue I want in that bag. There is one thing that no woman, and few men for that matter, regardless of station in life, is without in these days. It may be only the most tantalizing of clues which I shall be able to make nothing of, but I'll stake my reputation that it's there."

With no further explanation he threw back the cover of the bag, dropped on his knees before it, and dug into its contents. For several moments there was no sound save his eager breathing, echoed by the puffing breaths of Lamson, and the swishing of articles being hastily overturned in the bag. Then, with an almost explosive exhalation, he started back and sprang to his feet, three small articles in his hand.

"I have it, Lamson," he exclaimed. "I have it. Now, what can we make of it?"

He strode to the nearest window, with Lamson scuttling at his heels, and held up to the light three small, unmounted photographs. "You see, Lamson," he said, "every woman has a certain degree of sentiment in her make-up. Consequently, in these days of plentiful photographs, there is scarcely a woman anywhere who does not possess photographs of her early home, or associations surrounding it. Here we have the photographs, but, as they are not mounted, and bear no photographer's seal, their value to us will depend on our ability to recognize the places represented."

Lamson stared incredulously. "But my dear Sawyer," he protested, "those photographs may represent scenes hundreds or thousands of miles from here. How are we to recognize them?"

Quincy lowered the photographs and turned impressively. "Lamson," he said, "I have not yet looked at these photographs closely, but mark my words when I tell you that they will represent scenes within a radius of fifty miles. That woman was not a traveler."

Without further comment he raised the photographs once more and studied them carefully. The first depicted a woman, beyond doubt Mrs. Buck at a period much earlier in her life, standing before a small cottage of the style of architecture most frequently seen among the houses of the ocean fishermen. The second showed a large open boat, a trawler, fully manned, and lying just below a wharf with the wharf's buildings visible in the background. The last showed two fishermen standing on the steps of a hotel, and holding between them a strange monster of the deep, while, from above, curious guests, peered down from over the balcony rail.

"There, Lamson, I think we have our clue."

"But how? What in the deuce is there to all that stuff that shows you anything?" Lamson was fairly staggered with bewilderment.

"Look here!" Quincy flipped the second photograph into view. "That trawler indicates, as do all three photographs, a fishing community. Now look at the buildings in the background. On the central building you can dimly distinguish the sign of the fishing company: The Bay State Codfish Company. Now look at this third photograph. Above the fishermen's heads is the sign of the Puritan Hotel. By coupling those two names we have our clue. Both the Bay State Codfish Company and the Puritan Hotel are located in Gloucester. In the photograph of Mrs. Buck herself we find her standing before a typical fisherman's cottage. Therefore, does our clue not point toward Gloucester as a starting-point in our search for the woman's identity and that of her murderer? I also have another clue, but I shall leave that out of the matter for the present."

"Then you will go to Gloucester?" Lamson questioned.

"At once, although I would suggest that you do not mention the fact to the police. It might only serve to further muddle their brains, and they are sufficiently at sea in regard to this case already."

"You may use my car for the trip if you want to," Lamson volunteered immediately.

"No, I thank you. I prefer to go in the train. I shall be pleased to have your car take me to the station, though, if that will not inconvenience you."

As the pair descended the stairs they paused a moment to gaze at the activities of the police. The room remained in much the same condition as when they had originally viewed it, except for the fact that the body had been removed, thus doing away with the most gruesome feature of the case. Seeing them, the chief paused for a moment.

"Giving up so early in the game, Mr. Sawyer?" he inquired, a slightly sneering accent in his voice.

"Not exactly giving up, Chief," Quincy replied, ignoring the tone. "But my business temporarily calls me elsewhere, and, for the present, I shall be obliged to absent myself. I expect to return here later on, though, unless in the meantime you have been able to solve the mystery. You have found no trace of hidden wealth as yet, I suppose?"

"No, we have found nothing, but there must be some clue to it somewhere. I am about to act on your suggestion and search the cellar."

"Before you do that, Chief," said Quincy, smiling frankly, "I would suggest that you search the woman's chamber. There are some bank-books there which will be of interest to you."

"You mean that her money was deposited in a bank?" the chief demanded sharply.

"It was, and still is, in a bank, or in banks, to be more exact. I fear you will be wasting your time if you search farther for it here."

For a moment the chief stared silently, but at last a slow grin began to relieve the hard lines of his face. "Mr. Sawyer," he said, "you have put one across on us. I held you lightly in the beginning because, several times of late, my department has been considerably hindered by the actions of amateur detectives, and I took you to belong to the same class. I see you know your business, and I apologize for my former abruptness of speech."

The speech came as a complete surprise to Quincy, but he was not to be out-done in courtesy. "Chief," he said, "I accept your remarks in the spirit in which they were intended. Frankly, I am now starting out on a clue which I think will prove valuable. If I am successful I shall notify you of the fact on my return, and it is highly probable that we may be able to act together in the final scenes."

The chief regarded him with increased respect. "I shall be pleased to act with you if you are successful," he said simply.

In ten minutes' time Quincy was seated in Lamson's car and hurrying toward the railroad station. Shortly afterward he was aboard a train for Gloucester and, bending over the three photographs, was carefully arranging his plans for the campaign he intended to wage in that peculiar city.

All that day, and throughout the night, Lamson and the chief anxiously awaited the return of Quincy or the coming of some word which would indicate his progress. The affair by that time had been spread broadcast through the medium of the press, and the grounds swarmed with reporters, to the disgust of Lamson, who cordially hated the notoriety which was thus being brought to his door. The second forenoon following the murder passed away without result in the desired direction, and Lamson, unused to the necessary tedium of a police investigation, and suffering from the strain involved, was at his wits' end when Quincy suddenly reappeared as unostentatiously as he had departed. Lamson rushed eagerly from the house to greet him, the chief, no less eager, hurrying after, while the handful of reporters clustered around, listening intently for the first hint which might be incorporated in then several stories. Quincy waved them laughingly aside.

"Not yet, boys," he adjured them. "I have a good story for you, and you shall have it very shortly, but I must first make my report to Mr. Lamson."

Obediently the reporters fell back, accepting his assurance without question. Lamson and the chief reached him simultaneously and, above the hurried hum of the reporters' voices, rose Lamson's appeal:

"What luck, Sawyer? For heaven's sake tell me the result quickly."

Quincy took him soothingly by the arm. "It's settled, Lamson," he said quietly; "but my investigation has had a most remarkable result. A most surprising result! Come into the house, and I'll tell you all about it."

When they were seated in the library, or at least when the chief and Quincy were seated, Lamson being too nervous to do anything other than to fidget about the room, Quincy digressed slightly from the point of the matter in hand.

"I notice that you have gained considerable notoriety, Lamson," he said.

"Notoriety!" Lamson snorted the word furiously. "Notoriety! Yes, I certainly have, thanks to the press and its representatives outside! Look at the headlines which have been running. 'Wealthy Epicurean's Cook Murdered', 'Lamson's Elysium Wrecked by Murderer', and so on without end! Why in the world must I be dragged into the case in that manner?"

Quincy allowed himself a smile at Lamson's expense before proceeding. "You are merely the victim of circumstances, Lamson; but that was not what I intended to tell you. I wish to warn you that you are to receive still more notoriety because this case is about to produce one of the greatest sensations the press has had for years."

Lamson paled at the words, and his agitation increased perceptibly. "You don't mean," he stammered, "that you suspect me of the murder?"

"Oh, no, Lamson, great Scott, no!" Quincy hastened to assure him. "I have the murderer, and he has confessed. I merely wish to warn you that Mrs. Buck, regardless of her own identity, will still continue in the eyes of the public to be Lamson's cook, and as such she will be handled by the press. But sit down, man, nobody suspects you. I'll tell you my story at once, so that your mind may be placed at rest in that direction at least. You know of the photographs which I discovered before going to Gloucester?" he inquired, turning toward the chief.

"Yes, Mr. Lamson told me of them," the chief informed him.

"Very well, then, I wished you to know of them before telling my story, because I desire you to be in possession of the several clues which led me to Gloucester. As you are aware, one of those pictures showed the wharf of the Bay State Codfish Company. Now, Chief, remember. Do you not recall that the knife with which the murder was committed was stamped on the hilt with the letter 'B.S.C.Co.'? From that fact I argued that the person connected with the Bay State Codfish Company in whom Mrs. Buck was interested years ago must still be there, and that Gloucester was the spot which I must search for the murderer. As I said before, I found him; but in order to place you thoroughly in possession of the facts I am going to retrogress twelve years and begin my story at that point. The discovery of the man after I reached Gloucester was a very simple act, so simple as to hardly be worthy of recognition in the story, while his confession followed almost as a matter of course. He is at present being held by the Gloucester police. I recognized him, Lamson, from his photograph. He is the man on the right of that sea monster in the third picture; he also appears in the second photograph and, as the other does not, I naturally settled on him at once as the man whom I desired to find.

"But now for the story. Twelve years ago Amos Buck and his shrewish wife, Elizabeth—your cook, Lamson—lived in a small cottage at the far end of the Gloucester water-front. Amos was a trawler in the employ of the Bay State Codfish Company and, being a steady, temperate man, was regarded by the heads of his department as being one of their most reliable employees. But in his case, as in that of every other man, his home environment played a great part in the matter of his value to his employers. His wife's shrewish nature developed, and her constant nagging eventually began to play its part in his ultimate downfall, the result being that he finally became a steady patron of the nearest groggery, and it appeared that his complete degeneration would be merely a matter of time. Daily indulgence soon became protracted into sprees of a week's duration, and Mrs. Buck became more vituperative than ever.

"Then another link in the peculiar chain of circumstances was forged. Amos brought to his home a widowed cousin, Emma Bray by name, and insisted upon her taking up her permanent residence with himself and his wife. Mrs. Bray greatly resembled Mrs. Buck in figure, although their features were vastly dissimilar, and their dispositions were as far separated as the poles. The cousin proved to be a pleasant, even-tempered woman, and she showed every desire to alleviate the constant friction between Buck and his wife.

"Her attempts at intervention only added to Mrs. Buck's fury, and within a few weeks Mrs. Buck had developed a hatred for both her husband and his cousin that was almost inhuman in its intensity. The demeanor of his wife at last had its effect on Buck himself, and, instead of weakly submitting to her verbal assaults, as he had done in the past, he soon commenced to reply in kind, with the result that the house became a veritable inferno. This continued until one day Buck's temper, grown ragged from the constant warfare, gave way entirely and he struck his wife, knocking her down. Then, overcome by the deed, and by the scenes which had led up to it, he rushed from the house to his favorite haunt in a cheap saloon.

"Although naturally a reticent man, his tongue soon became loosened by liquor and, when one of his associates pointed to a fresh cut on the side of Buck's head, inquiring as to its origin, he replied that his wife had made it, but that he had fixed her so she wouldn't do it again. The savage look with which he accompanied the words, and the dark hint which seemed to be contained in them, caused the speech to be remembered. Shortly afterward Buck purchased a quart of raw rum and disappeared, going nobody knew where.

"The next morning he was aroused by the chief of police from the drunken slumber into which he had sunk behind the sheltering piles of a lumber wharf. The rough handling by the chief, together with the black looks and muttered threats of the small body of men who accompanied him, completely sobered Buck, and he demanded the reason of his arrest. The reply was unsatisfactory, being merely a gruff 'Guess you know', from the chief, and a volley of threats from the crowd, which was constantly growing larger.

"To Buck's surprise he was taken directly to his own house, and, when led indoors, the last trace of liquor was driven out of him, and his surprise was turned to horror. The main room of the cottage was indeed in a terrible state, its floor and walls being covered with blood, its meager furnishings broken and scattered, and its every appearance being as if a terrific battle had been waged within it. To make the nature of the crime which had been committed doubly sure, a bloodstained axe lay at one side of the room, where it had evidently been thrown by the fleeing murderer. But, whatever hopes the chief may have had of securing a confession from Buck by taking him to the place were speedily dashed, for Buck, instead of breaking down, appeared too utterly stupefied by the scene for speech of any kind.

"No trace of either woman had been found, and there was consequently nothing to do save to hold Buck on suspicion while the search for the bodies was being conducted. The search speedily bore fruit, for, within an hour of Buck's arrest, the body of a woman was found floating in the harbor. The features had been obliterated, being so badly hacked and battered as to make recognition impossible, but the clothing on the body was speedily identified as being that of Mrs. Buck. As no trace of the cousin was found it was decided that her body must have floated out to sea on the tide, and Buck was held, charged with the murder of both women.

"At the trial circumstantial evidence figured strongly in securing Buck's conviction, but there was also a beautiful train of circumstantial evidence in his favor. He pointed out that no blood-stains had been found on his clothing, and defied the prosecution to demonstrate a way in which he could have hacked a body as his wife's had been mangled and then have conveyed it to the water without having become stained with blood. He also showed a streak of genius by defying the police to show conclusively that his cousin, Emma Brat, was really dead, as no trace of her body had been found. This part of the indictment was shortly dropped, and he stood accused of only the one murder, that of his wife.

"Of course his rash words in the saloon played an important part against him, but in his favor was the absence of bloodstains upon him and that fact, together with his drunkenness and the well-known frequency with which his wife had assaulted him, both orally and physically, saved him from execution. He was, however, convicted of murder in the second degree, and sentenced to imprisonment for life; but, even after Buck had been imprisoned, there remained many people who did not believe him guilty of the crime. Consequently, after he had served a term of years, a movement was set on foot to have him pardoned, the movement being eventually successful.

"After his release Buck returned to Gloucester and quietly resumed his old life, taking up his residence in his former house and again entering the employ of the Bay State Codfish Company. For two years he lived quietly and then, like a sudden thunderclap, came a piece of news which entirely upset his every thought. An associate came to him, giving him positive assurance that he had seen Mrs. Buck in Beverly, and had been told that she was employed by a rich man as a cook. For days Buck brooded over that information, striving to make himself realize that he had not only been sent to prison for a crime which he had never committed, but also for one which, possibly, had never been committed at all.

"At last he could stand the strain no longer, and so set out one night for Beverly, to prove for himself the truth or falsity of the weird rumor. Before starting, moved by some instinct which even he himself cannot define, he secreted one of the company's knives in his coat, giving it no more thought after his departure from Gloucester.

"On his arrival in Beverly he had no difficulty in locating Lamson's estate and, proceeding here at once, he slipped about in the darkness, searching for the woman who might or might not prove to be his wife. He soon stumbled on the cook's cottage, and, peering through one of the lighted windows, he was able to clearly view the woman within and his feelings cannot be described when he realized that she was indeed his wife. Overcome by a blind, insensate fury, he made his way quickly to the front of the house, burst open the door and confronted her.

"According to his story the woman showed no surprise at seeing him, but merely sat staring into his face with a smile of contempt on her lips. She made no reply when he accused her of allowing him to be falsely imprisoned, but continued to gloat over him with an air that aroused his already nearly uncontrollable fury to a pitch which it had never hitherto reached. He broke into savage denunciation of her, and, at last, stung her into replying to his charges. To his intense surprise she admitted them to be true. Not only that, but she boastfully asserted that she had killed his cousin out of revenge, and had then dressed the body in her own clothes to throw suspicion on him, had dragged it into the water and had then fled from the place in disguise. As she warmed up to the recital she added almost fiendish details, and through it all she continued to glory in her own success and Buck's resulting conviction.

"Naturally such a scene could have but one ending. Buck's temper became more and more savage and at the conclusion of her story he had reached a point but little, if anything, short of insanity. He told her he was going to kill her and that he would be justified in the act. The announcement sobered her and silenced her tongue; but, instead of screaming for help as he had expected her to do, she launched herself fiercely at his throat. You know the result. The struggle was short-lived, and at its conclusion Buck hurried from the place, making his way immediately back to Gloucester, where I found him.

"Now, gentlemen," and with the words Quincy straightened impressively, "now we come to the sensational part of the whole affair. The question to be decided, and it is an important one, is: *Can Buck he punished for the murder?*

"At first glance the natural reply would be that he can; but, can he? Can the courts touch him in any way? When a man is tried and acquitted he cannot again be brought to trial for the same offence, even though it may afterwards be shown conclusively that he is guilty. Therefore, can Buck be twice punished for the same offence? He has already paid the penalty, has paid in advance, so to speak, for the privilege of killing his wife. He was convicted when innocent, and, now that he is guilty, can he be again convicted of the same crime for which he has already paid the penalty which was legally demanded of him?

"I freely admit, gentlemen, that it is a question which I cannot answer, and you may rest assured that the press will eagerly await the decision of the Supreme Court if it is considered necessary to carry the matter that far."